Also by Ellis Sharp

Novels

The Dump
Unbelievable Things
Walthamstow Central
Intolerable Tongues
Lamees Najim

Short Fiction

The Aleppo Button
Lenin's Trousers
(with Mac Daly) *Engels on Video*
To Wanstonia
Driving My Baby Back Home
Aria Fritta
Quin Again and other stories
Dead Iraqis: Selected Short Stories

Non-Fiction

Sharply Critical

ELLIS SHARP

TO WETUMPKA

Zoilus Press

A Zoilus Press paperback
First published in Great Britain by Zoilus Press in 2015
Reprinted 2019

A CIP catalogue record for this book is available from the British
Library.

ISBN 9781902878966

Jacket photographs by the Mr Triangle Agency

Cover design by The Ever-Shifting Subject

Typeset by Electrograd

ZOILUS PRESS
York, England

To Wetumpka

for Anna and Andrew

Part One

THE END never is.

Tollinger woke up to it. All this. The pressing need for something to happen. A different future.

He lay for a while in a fold of white sheets. There was a smell of dust and vellum and old furniture. Experimentally, Tollinger moved his limbs. He squirmed and twisted and scowled, wrinkly as a newborn.

His face seemed to cloud over. There were times when he truly believed he didn't stand the ghost of a chance. He'd been running on empty for as long as he could remember. Night after night he had weird dreams. Bad dreams. In this latest one, in the dark corner by the door, there was either a small animal or a huge insect. For a long time it didn't move, and then, just once, its pale spine seemed to ripple like water. It was about the size of a paperback novella. Its body was covered in fur like a bumble bee but it had the horns of a giant beetle. The creature made no move to attack. In the end Tollinger decided to leave. He walked quickly past it and out through the door. Beyond lay a tunnel lit by a dim, reddish light.

Maybe it was time to go see the gypsy, who was staying in that big hotel on the other side of town. Maybe not. Tollinger woke up. He made himself coffee. He wanted a different kind of dream. A frenzy he'd come out of, say, like Popeye Doyle in *French Connection II*.

Tollinger quit the great city, heading first the other way, then north by north-east. Perhaps, he thought, he was imagining hayfields and barrens. Maybe he wanted the pattern of his nights broken, so that one day he'd wake up in a New York apartment where a telephone rang out from the bedroom, stinging him like some nasty metallic kind of gnat. He wondered if he'd read somewhere about a fractured assemblage of trivialities caught in the advance light of a great event. He conceived of a possible resemblance to that poet whose mind worked with astonishing rapidity in the final illness. It was not delirium. The greater part of those waking hours were passed in rapid soliloquies on a variety of subjects, the chain of which, from his imperfect utterance, those who attended to them were quite unable to follow. Yet in no instance – except in a final lapse of memory – was discovered the least irrationality.

At length, decisively, Tollinger holed up on the coast, in Lowestoft. There was no risk of him running into anyone he knew in that town. It was at the edge of nothing much, leaning out into the grey North Sea. Metal signs placed around the town warned that you could go no further east in the kingdom than this.

Lowestoft was the kind of place that dreamed of being somewhere else. Vancouver, maybe. No one he knew would ever be seen dead in Lowestoft. It just wasn't their kind of place. He knew he could start again here. Begin a whole new story, against a grey background. Here he was freed as far as was possible from the end of love, the cold presence of death, the thinning of friendship. He could begin at last to efface, expunge, erase, delete and hopefully move towards a different last page to the one previously planned. Along the way he might hope for the stimulus of fresh adventures and some awesome pictorial detail. *Hope*. A four-letter word derived from the Late Old English *hopa*, corresponding to the Old Low German *tōhopa* and the Dutch *hoop*. One who is hoping might be found *soaring* and *starry-eyed*. Such a character might be *would-be*.

Tollinger was confident no one among the population would recognise him in Lowestoft even though, once, briefly, he'd been keyboard player and trumpeter in The Mal Kontents. The band had had one hit – "The Hole in Me". Later, following five flops in a row, the group fell apart. After they disintegrated, they vanished into their individual obscurities and became old and shadowy. This was true of Tollinger too. He no longer looked like a once-upon-a-time MalK. Now his scalp was

8

entirely different. His face – it was undeniable – was beginning to melt. Limpness and waste had somehow managed to stick to his days. In the mirror, below his armpits, he saw the rippled skin of a lizard.

Tollinger liked Lowestoft. It was at the end of something. The factories were derelict. There were numerous vacant plots. Beside rotting warehouses weeds spurted from fissures in plateaus of concrete desolation. The grey everywhere incubated tropical adjectives. The old harbour was a desolation of empty quays and shuttered buildings. Windowless structures and gates and high fencing shut you out.

A wind was always blowing. Always a low remote roar, which might have been traffic along a faraway freeway, or an ocean fringed with quiet furies. Metaphors clanked in the night, shadowing rolling Coke cans. Soon after Tollinger arrived there was a bad storm. The sea came over the harbour wall. It washed around Station Square and flooded shops in the High Street.

Some days, when the sky was paper white, clouds of corvids moved around in the space above the town like whirled specks of ash from a big industrial fire.

Once, a big crater appeared without warning in the road which passed by the station. It was filled in, but later others appeared randomly around the town.

If he had to, Tollinger knew he could wait out the time quite happily in this place. The sound of a harmonium reached his ears. It was someone like himself, playing a Nico album with the window wide open. Quite possibly, like himself, they felt a special affinity with certain words. Silk, perfume, pallid, marble, relinquish, for example. Temporal, nocturnal, central, wept, index.

Tollinger didn't know how long it would take to begin all over again. For a long time he'd felt flat and used-up. Almost as though he was due to die. Depleted was the word. It was his heart, you see. What's the bloody use of developing the cardiograms? Like an old gag-man, intolerable tongues tormented him, but few listened, few heard. Still, he was

9

fortunate. He'd enough to get by on for at least one more year. Plus there was a trickle of royalties from the old hit. They still played it on the radio. Hungry new generations bought the last album, which defrauded purchasers with a GREATEST HITS label.

Twelve months were probably adequate. Long enough for sweet Lady Luck to take him on elsewhere – to a new heart, a new home, a fresh beginning in another landscape. A different, better narrative. Multitudes, multitudes: soldiers, doctors, nurses, taxis, drivers of jeeps, in a heat the hue of a yellow dream. The sky an inverted bowl of fleckless pale blue broken only about twelve degrees above one horizon by a light so glaring that it was difficult to look at. Plus the soothing accompaniment of slow gentle piano music and muted strings. And adjectives, many adjectives.

It was good to move on, good to discover a new dimension. You are always nearer by not keeping still. He was sickened by his trudge, which had become mechanical as he passed through the evening streets. He turned things over in his mind but they returned like rinsed socks, requiring heat before they became usable again.

Before he left the big city Tollinger had given away most of his possessions. He took them to charity shops. Tollinger felt better without objects. He needed to lose the weight of anchors. Naturally, realistically, he needed strong verbs and a certain quantity of nouns, but he could do without stuff like that pinewood chest of drawers or the television. They chained you to a particular room. As for all the books and DVDs, he could always them buy again, if he ever felt like revisiting them. Besides, the technology was archaic. Everything was out there in a cloud, if he ever wanted to reconnect.

The fridge he'd donated to the Red Cross. It was another monstrous possession. Bloated and heavy. It made intermittent odd little scratchy gargling sounds which rubbed like sandpaper against his mind during the silence of the long afternoons and the solitude of his nights. He was glad to be free of that vexatious structure. It was like giving away a copy of a much acclaimed novel, in the certain knowledge he'd never want to read it again. Also, defrosting it was a tedious chore, which he always resented and left too late.

Free of the heavy furniture of a thinning first-draft relationship, he was free to move on. But he wasn't sure how far or fast he could go before some flashbacks caught up with him. He felt they might be waiting to appear when he least expected it. A flashback can be useful in explaining obscurities of motivation or identity, he thought, suddenly remembering being alone on the sofa, staring at a large flatscreen, watching *Lost*. But he also remembered that memories can be false. He knew that from the time skinny Emily had persuaded him to watch *Blade Runner* and *Total Recall*.

The corner of a curtain was restless. The sky sagged with drifts of grey. It was trying to snow. It soon gave up.

Tollinger watched a movie released in the final quarter of the last century. It was bright with stars but curiously lacklustre. Jack Nicholson did his sly manic Jack Nicholson grin. Other famous faces looked sombre. In one scene a young Robert de Niro was sat in a car at with an actress Tollinger didn't recognise.

"Listen."

"What?"

"Nothing."

It was the best moment in a film that never caught fire.

That first morning in Lowestoft, when he went out, Tollinger had to step over a dead seagull. The gull was lying on its side in the alley. Up close, it seemed enormous. There was nothing to indicate what had killed it. The only movement was around its thick throat, where its pure white plumage was disturbed by the wind. Later, in random places around the town, he came across more dead birds. A robin on a soot-black verge, its head resting on a leaf. A blackbird on its back beside a kerb. A starling which had lost its sparkle. The origin of their termination was obscure.

The wind was blowing like mad. It felt icy and hard. It came in from the east, across the German Ocean. The Ocean had been deleted in the 1914 text but Tollinger decided to reinstate it. Knowing nothing of where he really was, he felt free.

A day after the interpolation the wind was still blowing like mad. It swept past the mute Bird's Eye factory and funnelled up the alley. Scraps of silver litter danced at its passing. It tugged at the dead gull, trying to shake it back to life.

As if propelled by some invisible force Tollinger walked around, exploring. He could still feel that wind. It came whirling down the side streets and rummaged under his shirt. It was as inescapable as a symbol in a set text.

The town was shabby and impoverished. The people looked poor. The shopping centre had cancer. The bus station was cramped and dismal. Cars trailing fumes flowed everywhere like slow-moving sewage. Handcuffed to the steering wheels were deformed lobsters.

There was a shop which sold second-hand goods. A radio, labelled "DOES NOT WORK BUT NOT BROKEN". A set of carousel wheels for projecting holiday slides. A pair of old, wrinkled boots once worn by a Dutchman, size 10. A second-hand light bulb, for the especially stricken.

The harbour pier was a banal slab of concrete jutting out alongside a grey dreary industrial lagoon. A solitary fisherman stood by a pair of rods, staring morosely at the oily water. He was there most days. Tollinger never saw him catch anything.

One day Tollinger discovered fencing blocking the pier entrance. The fisherman was no longer there. A notice attached to the mesh explained that the pier had been closed for reasons of safety.

Tollinger's monochrome low-rent apartment occupied half the top floor of a decayed old house imagined beside one of the Scores, as they were called. The Scores were narrow alleys which dropped steeply from the town's main street to the harbour below. In their cramped, walled-in desolation you could score. Lowestoft had a drugs problem, it was said. Not true. Lowestoft had a drugs solution. You could even get LSD.

Forget about E's and wizz. Oh boy! Onwards into the interior! La vuelta al día en ochenta mundos! In more senses than one, senõr!

Tollinger fell out of bed, repeatedly. He dragged a comb across his head, repeatedly. The frames were quivering slightly. The light was uncertain. Fever perhaps? Quite possibly. While over there, do you see? Down there. A gigantic wind turbine sprouts from the midst of the drab harbour buildings. It resembles a strange metal parasite, thriving amidst industrial waste.

Lowestoft bore no resemblance at all to the scenes in the heritage photographs which hung on the walls of The Joseph Conrad.

Yes, Lowestoft was the place for Tollinger. When the North Sea gales blew in, the blades of the slowly turning turbine swished and went faster and faster. At full speed they sent a low drilling whine through the long nights. The turbine was named Gulliver. Alcohol and nightly fistfuls of barbiturates numbed Gulliver's presence. By midnight everything was as black as the ninth plague of Egypt.

In the afternoons, in this part of town, there was the sound of throbbing music and raucous drinking. Girls sat on kerbs, queasy. Many had fat thighs and laddered stockings. Sometimes they vomited, while their friends laughed.

Half a mile to the south, across the street from The Joseph Conrad, stood the dark station. The trains went only in two directions, to places where Tollinger had no desire to go. He'd lost the will to visit cities.

Time passed.

How delightful it would be to spend a whole day on the beach, lost in dreams! But the charms of inertia and slow decay were starting to lose some of their lustre. Better would be to drive along the shore road four times, becoming a different person on each trip. It was on his tongue to ask what this meant. There were moments when he was tempted to take the shore road back to where he'd started from and await developments. But for that he'd need an auto.

It was undeniable. Cabin fever was beginning to make him restless and wild. *Where to now?* thought the central character at the beginning of Chapter Four in the translated novella which lay on the table in the kitchenette. The jacket of the paperback was illustrated by a detail from Gustav Klimt's *The Bride.* The introduction, by a once popular commercial novelist who was nowadays little read, asserted that at the centre of the novella author's art and life lay a *solemn playfulness.* The translated text had been transformed into a screenplay and the screenplay had been translated into a movie, which Tollinger recalled he had not particularly liked. It had gone on too long, the dialogue was lacklustre, and the stars had not shone all that brightly.

He finished the novella and turned to a second-hand five shillings Mayflower-Dell paperback he'd bought for a couple of coins in a gloomy little bric-a-brac-stuffed shop at the decayed end of the High Street. The pages were baked brown by sunlight and the cover was as wrinkled as Samuel Beckett.

The title and author's name were superimposed at a slant upon the voluptuous rump of a naked black woman. The book promised an account of a famous American novelist's red-blooded true-life adventures, involving card-playing, ferocious argument, swearing, fist-fights and memorable encounters with *men "gone bamboo".*

Intrigued (for Tollinger had never before come across this last expression) he glanced at the book's preface. The famous American novelist – whom Tollinger had heard of but never read – abused other famous contemporaries "whose harsh artistry has flattened into smooth profundity". But in a world of tepid conformity there were still those prepared to take risks.

Rap the novelist's disorderly lair – "You in there! What are you up to now? What's next?"

You-In-There doesn't know what he's up to at midnight, 0230 hours, nor upon the gong of noon. He drives a collision course, lights out, along an untraveled way.

Tollinger decided it was time to consult an Ordnance Survey map.

Two days later he stood at the bus stop by the diseased bus station. He boarded a 61 bus that arrived seventeen minutes later than the advertised time. Its side panels were the colour of soot-speckled vomit. Tollinger was the only passenger. The tropically hot bus travelled across central Lowestoft in a sequence of erratic spasms – a sudden, jolting halt, then a throbbing, drawn-out pause, then a quick desperate gasp from the wheels as they rushed forwards with a dream of perpetual motion. And then the next abrupt, lurching stop. It was like being inside a machine designed to illustrate the processes involved in a heart seizure. Terminal cardiac arrest could not be far off.

This last illusion was reinforced by the sight of the sluggish river of vehicles ahead coming to a standstill as the wings of the Bascule Bridge unfolded in the distance. A section of carriageway rose vertically and became immobile. Red lights flashed urgently along a barrier.

There was a long wait. It was like arriving too early for a cremation at Stonefall. You sit in silence, waiting for the hearse. Nothing moves. Ranks of gravestones stretch away on all sides. You are left with your thoughts. That great triptych painted on oak slides, as though on castors, into your mind. Two wings enclose a panel teeming with energetic nudes. Zoom in and observe extraordinary spectacles. The densely populated landscapes darken and vanish as the wings are folded. Once the wings have closed the backsides display a grisaille sphere of uncertain significance.

On the outskirts of the town was a grey circular water tower, a magic mushroom twinned with a roundabout coated in dead vegetation. Further down the road, in the distance, could be seen the forlorn huts of a Holiday Camp. Arranged in stark lines and surrounded by a high mesh fence, they bore a distinct resemblance to the accommodation supplied at a concentration camp.

A rickety structure erected in a field displayed the bridge and flaking eyewires of a giant pair of glasses. One painted disc had dropped away, leaving only a single yellowish-grey retina to cast a jaundiced gaze at passers-by. A large section of the board concealing the scaffold had fallen away, leaving behind an amputated message: GET YOU.

As it receded behind the bus, which had now achieved a dizzying 40 mph, the eye seemed to close up and briefly wink at Tollinger. But this was plainly some kind of illusion, to be filed alongside sightings of a wild lion in Essex and a mysterious big cat outside Arlecdon. Unless, of course, the cat and the lion were inter-dimensional travellers, in which case the impact of the paranormal might well extend into the drearier parts of Suffolk. But Tollinger did not believe in that lion or the enlarged cat.

Tollinger went as far as Kessingland, just down the coast. The bus, diverted by roadworks, halted briefly by a parked car to wait for an oncoming lorry.

"I can hear lions," Tollinger said to the driver.

The driver explained there was a safari park behind the trees. *Africa Alive!* The lions were roaring in their enclosure.

The driver dropped him at the end of Rider Haggard Lane. From there it's a short walk to the beach.

Tollinger followed the road through an estate of modern brick bungalows. Beside a grass verge he saw a badger. It lay on its side, perfectly still. He had never seen a badger before, except in photographs and wildlife documentaries. But it wasn't asleep, it was dead. There was no obvious injury but some flies had gathered in an excited cloud around the badger's neck.

He came to a caravan park. The symmetry of the lined-up trailers reminded Tollinger of the Holiday Camp. This reiterated pattern squeezed out a trio of flashbacks. "K-Z" it said on the single decker bus parked outside the little rail station long ago. It was there for the tourists. What was most memorable of all from that day was what had preceded it. The soft announcement as the train pulled out of the terminus in Munich. A list of suburban destinations, including the softly articulated "Dachau". To those stolid regular commuters its resonance was blunted. There was no difference to the tone of the guard speaking into the PA system on Tollinger's old regular train from Waterloo. "This train will be stopping at Woking, Guildford, Haslemere, Petersfield, Havant, Fratton, Portsmouth and Southsea, and Portsmouth Harbour."

Beyond the caravans the settlement's dog walkers began to fade along the shingle.

2

SOON TOLLINGER had the beach to himself. It is hard work, walking across shingle. He crunched southward. The sky was manganese blue. The sea was grey. It did not look wet. It resembled paper which has dried out and become wrinkled after being soaked.

Ahead of him was a wood, rising behind a small cliff. Coastal erosion had caused some of the trees to fall over the edge. The trunks and stumps of dead trees littered the shingle. They were smooth and plausible, these salt-scoured wooden shapes.

Something dark bobbed up in the water.

At first Tollinger assumed it was a lump of wood or possibly a dog. It was just a few yards from the shore, at the fringe of his vision. Then the head vanished.

He expected it to surface again but it didn't.

Puzzled, he walked on. Across the blank sky a contrail began to stretch out behind a silent moving scrap of punctuation.

Far out on the horizon half a dozen tankers were anchored. He'd heard they were waiting for the price of oil to rise on the world's markets.

Three or four minutes later a dark, glistening shape briefly broke surface just a few yards offshore. It resembled a hump.

It happened again, twice, then disappeared.

Tollinger realised what he'd seen was a seal. This was obviously a stray from one of the colonies of seals that he'd read lived at certain points along the Norfolk coast.

He walked on.

The headland seemed oddly sinister. Most of the trees were dying. Their wrinkled bark had a bleached pallor. Many were leaning at a sharp angle, reminiscent of the aftermath of the great explosion at Tunguska. They stirred a distant memory of paragraphs by H.P. Lovecraft.

One tree, perfectly vertical, protruded incongruously from the waves. Lovers had carved their initials in the bark.

At the rear of the beach, at the edge of his perception, a small object broke into a run. It was the size of a rat. It ran on, paused as if for breath, then accelerated again. Finally it stopped, like a narrative.

There was no tail and the object was a little fuzzy. It wasn't a rat. Tollinger went over to see what it was. As he drew nearer he saw that it was a sort of green-brown seaweed. He picked it up. It wasn't slimy at all but dry and fluffy, like a clump of hair. On the underside was a shimmer of pink. It was sea fern, delicate and light. The way it moved resembled tumbleweed in an American movie. But it was much smaller than tumbleweed.

There were more clumps of the material in the vicinity. They had evidently been deposited there at high tide. From time to time some of the other clumps were lifted by the wind and went scampering across the shingle. The momentary resemblance to the rodents Tollinger had often seen in the great city was striking.

Beyond the headland's bulge Tollinger came to a small lagoon. It was separated from the ocean by a bank of shingle. As he crunched his way along this pebbly crest he came upon the remains of buildings and structures. There were slices of brick smoothed as flat as sole. Broken fragments of tiles. Bits of light brown sewer pipe. These turd-coloured fragments made Tollinger think of Beppo the circus clown. Before he took up clowning the man in the gigantic slippers had been a professional diver. Once he descended from a yacht in Loch Ness. The water was very dark. Suddenly he came up against some slime. It was pale grey and stretched out like a ribbon.

Beppo dived to avoid it. I got a very strange, cold feeling on me, he said afterwards. It was a very eerie feeling all the time I was going down. I had the impression I was being watched, by what or who I can't say. This strange feeling became an obsession with me. I found it very difficult to get away from this slime.

After returning to the surface he decided it would be better to become a circus clown. He changed his name to Beppo. As a clown you are part of a crowd. People laugh at you but they like you. It's a good feeling, falling flat on your face in sawdust while people hoot and cheer.

Tollinger went on.

On this stretch of beach, apart from shards and sections of pipe, there were big ragged chunks of concrete. Some had pebbles sunk in them. Some were embedded with rusty mesh patterned like a crossword puzzle. These were all evidently remnants of structures undermined by the sea.

And then what happened, happened.

Something moved in the water to his right. It started wriggling in the shallows.

Tollinger wondered if it was an eel. The lagoon had been formed by a flood tide, and he guessed that the creature had been trapped there when the tide had receded.

Tollinger had never liked eels. There was something brutish and bellicose about their appearance. He'd tried eating one once and it tasted vile.

He threw a stone in the general direction of the ripples on the surface. At once the disturbance died away and the surface became calm. He wondered if he'd hit the creature on the head and stunned it, or even killed it. But probably not, most probably he'd simply scared it.

He stood a yard or so from the edge, waiting and watching.

The wind sent fresh ripples across the surface, making it impossible to see whatever was in this shallow trough of water. It was all dappled and jerky.

After a minute, there was another swirl of water. This time Tollinger was more ambitious. He found a lump of ragged concrete the size and weight of a couple of bricks. He raised it up, level with his brow, and hurled it into the water. It landed with a terrific splash.

Tollinger was enjoying himself. This was the kind of fun he'd had as a child, when his parents took him to the seaside. The simple pleasure of throwing stones into the sea – sometimes at a bobbing bottle, sometimes simply for the sheer excitement of seeing how far he could throw a stone. He recalled that sensuous *plop!* as the pebble hit the surface and sank from view. One rare occasions he'd hit the neck of a bobbing bottle and feel a great sense of triumph as it cracked open and sank.

The ripples subsided.

Behind him the waves grated against the shingle, an ancient frottage.

It began to cloud over.

This little game was starting to bore him.

He decided to send one more missile into the miniature lake before going on his way. He selected a pair of broken house bricks.

They were ruddy-coloured, as if freshly baked. Cemented together, they resembled pieces from a giant's jigsaw puzzle.

Balanced in the palm of his hand, the twinned bricks swayed a moment beside his shoulder and then shot off along their brief trajectory. Their passage would have looked good in slow-mo, he reflected. And the arrival at the intended destination.

A new thought flashed across his mind: that this was like a miniature Hiroshima – a huge cataclysm in a tiny world. A spout of water rose up satisfyingly high, sending a big surging wave out to the shores of this inland sea. The spout collapsed and spattered the surface, adding to the turbulence.

That will teach you, eel, he thought.

The surface settled down again. The wind had dropped and the surface was flat calm, like a mirror. He stared into the depths, looking for the eel. But now the sun had come out again and the surface was as impenetrable as the blue-grey sky it reflected. He could see a few large submerged dark pebbles around the rim, nothing more.

It was time to go. The atmosphere had become close, as if a

storm was imminent. The air felt treacly and sticky and oppressive. Out at sea the sky had turned yellowish, and cumulonimbus was starting to billow up. The line of oil tankers looked like a row of tombs.

And then it happened.

There was a stirring in the shallows, as if the sediment at the bottom had been disturbed. A sandy swirl.

The surface of the water broke into an ever-expanding line.

Something was swimming fast towards the spot where he stood.

Tollinger was too surprised to do anything but stare. He might have been at Foyers, stupefied and helpless.

The line cutting across the surface moved towards the precise spot where he was standing. He glimpsed a slender shape, of no particular colour.

A small head broke the surface. It was the head of a snake, smooth, rounded, hard, with a pattern of sandy-coloured scales which seemed to shimmer with movement, as if each scale was a muscle. If you press the fingers and thumbs of one hand together to make an arrow head – well, that was about the size of the head of this creature.

Embedded in this snake-like head were two dark slits, which framed two slashes of faint, fiery yellow.

Tollinger had the distinct sensation that this strange creature was looking up at him.

He stumbled back a pace or so, unnerved. Tollinger had never heard of such a creature like this in a place as mild and domesticated as Suffolk. But somewhere deep in his mind a perception formed that this was a creature of the deep, of some faraway exotic location, which had somehow found its way to an English coast.

He recalled that on the news lately there had been items about how ocean currents were in flux around the globe, with huge expanses of algae appearing in the Mediterranean, and exotic fish following new currents of warmth to beaches which were previously cold and inhospitable.

This was a foreign fish, no doubt.

It had been tossed into this little patch of water by a high tide, and been trapped here. It was waiting to be reunited with the sea.

That theory collapsed the next instant as the snake flicked its back and came out of the water completely. It was *an amphibian.*

Tollinger retreated another couple of paces, then stopped. He felt a slight paralysis of shock, thickened by a growing sense of disgust, even fear. Throwing stones into a pool of water had seemed a harmless and safe occupation. Now that the water-snake was exposed to view, and on land, it presented itself as a much easier target. But he felt strangely vulnerable.

Are water snakes venomous? Tollinger had no idea but he didn't feel like throwing anything more, just in case it somehow managed to bite him.

To his horror, the creature began to slither towards him. This was worse than a movie. When its tail was out of the water he saw that it was, in all, at least a yard long. Its torso was considerably thinner than its head and was of a pale blue. Along the edges were silvery fringes of membrane, which he assumed were for propelling itself underwater.

The movements of the sea-snake were slow and languorous. It was a dream creature. It moved towards Tollinger, quite unafraid. But, weirdly, unlike a crawling snake, it held its head up, perhaps twelve inches or so.

The posture gave it an unmistakeably threatening appearance.

He decided to retreat. It was perhaps shameful, even a little cowardly, to be running away from what was, after all, some simple organism of very limited intelligence. Yet in the watches of the night Hemingway himself had heard retreat beaten.

Tollinger decided to put a safe distance between himself and the creature, then pelt it with stones. He'd scare it back into its watery home, then go on his way.

A low rise of shingle separated the lagoon from the main beach, and he ran to the crest of this ridge and stopped. When Tollinger looked back he expected to have put at least ten yards between himself and the exotic intruder. To his amazement it was only about two yards away. It had moved almost as fast as he had.

That settled the matter. He decided to run. Tollinger turned and sprinted along the ridge, heading south, to the nearest civilisation.

He ran some twenty yards as fast as he could, then, without stopping, glanced back.

This was when the affair became quite simply terrifying. The sea-snake had increased its speed and was moving across the shingle in a sequence of rapid flicks of its body. It remained just a couple of yards behind him, its head still raised high. Its eye slits regarded him with an unmistakeably malevolent intensity.

Tollinger felt indignant and a little angry, as well as fearful. It is a ridiculous thing for a fully grown man – a representative, after all, of a species which built Stonehenge without cranes, not to mention the Pyramids, and which has put men on the moon – to be humiliatingly chased by a much smaller, flimsy *thing* of very limited intellect.

Tollinger also felt a strong sense that the media had let him down. Surely creatures which spend their whole lives in the depths of the ocean cannot possibly see in the way that *Homo sapiens* can? He had read articles, watched documentaries, and listened to zoologists on the breakfast show. He had watched David Attenborough's programmes. The name Darwin was not entirely alien to him. He'd even once read his Penguin Classic, though he remembered almost nothing of its contents. Once, in a flush of enthusiasm, he had even visited Glen Roy.

The fact remained that Tollinger was being chased along a beach in Suffolk by a creature which seemed determined to defy accepted scientific knowledge. And he felt completely certain that those narrow burning reptilian eyes were watching him.

Or was he deluding himself? Perhaps it was responding not to sight but to sound. He was, after all, on a shingle beach. Every step he took created a loud muddy scrunching noise. A blind man could have chased him without difficulty.

Tollinger wondered how he could outwit the beast, and then realised.

Run down to the rushing water's edge!

He scrambled down the far side of the ridge and reached the sea's edge. The waves quietly slapped the beach, indifferent to the drama being played out there.

He ran into the shallows and paused. The snake stopped and seemed to be watching. Had he outwitted it? Tollinger walked slowly along in the surf, parallel to the beach. If the creature responded to sound, his presence would be lost amid the general crash and rolling of the waves.

Bad idea.

The snake simply kept pace with Tollinger, moving sideways along the beach, just a couple of metres offshore. Worse, it had now caught up with him and put itself between him and the beach. It seemed to have no obvious ill intent but its appearance and behaviour made him uneasy. It seemed to want to keep him company. But to what end?

Tollinger frowned. There was one shred of comfort. He couldn't work out why the creature didn't simply enter the water. Once back in its natural element it would be able to move much faster than him.

A possible reason for its tactic soon became clear.

To Tollinger's horror, his options were rapidly narrowing. Ahead of him a stream cut across the beach between two embankments of sand, emptying into the sea. As he drew near he saw that the volume of water, and the depth, made crossing it impossible. He could have gone deeper into the sea and tried swimming past this obstacle but that did not seem viable. For a start, to attempt swimming while fully clothed, wearing shoes, would have been foolish. Tollinger knew that the currents off this beach were strong. To plunge in fully clothed would be inviting death by drowning.

The alternative of stripping off his coat, shirt, trousers and shoes, was altogether too drastic. Even assuming he could get round to the other side while holding a bundle of sodden clothing, he would simply end up very wet and very cold. And even if he managed it, Tollinger had a horrible feeling the snake would be waiting for him on the far side. Or, worse – much worse, and much more probable – it would simply slide into the sea after him. It would finish him off before he was anywhere near to getting past the stream.

The situation, like the late stage of his relationship with Emily, was hopeless. His spirits were now at a very low ebb. He cursed himself for ever disturbing this vexatious creature in the first place. He was now almost at the stream and it was as if the snake was enjoying his predicament. It had sidled along to just below the first of the sandy embankments and was resting there, half curled, head upright, swaying and watching intently. Tollinger shivered. It reminded him very much of how a cat waits patiently for a nearby bird on a lawn. The cat crouches, motionless, eyes burning, its muscles tight with anticipation.

Tollinger realised, sick at heart, that there was only one real option. He would have to go up the beach and deal with this thing. He'd arm himself with as many large stones as he could find. Then he'd go towards it, get close, and pelt it with them. He would smash the brute's head open and break its back. And if he missed and it came up to him he'd stamp on it with his shoe. He'd stamp on it and stamp on it until it was broken and oozing beneath him. And then he would walk away and leave the tide to dispose of its strands of glistening filth.

That is what he would do.

So, decided, he came out of the water and began picking up the biggest stones he could find.

The snake, which was now a few yards away, watched Tollinger impassively. It was a thing with a very tiny, narrow brain. It could not hope to outwit a brain which had the benefit of inheriting the evolutionary advantages of thousands of years of human life on a planet full of danger. Man had tamed the dog, the horse and now the solar system. A snake was no match for a man on a beach in Suffolk.

By now Tollinger had assembled an arsenal consisting of six large stones balanced in the palm of his left hand. He had a seventh, a bigger one, in his right fist.

He stepped forward to do battle.

3

A VOICE spared him the ordeal.

A woman's voice, shouting something. A name, Tollinger thought.

Something appeared on the sand embankment to his left. A black head, moving. A dog, a black and white dog. It saw Tollinger and began barking.

He heard the sound of someone scrunching along the shingle and a moment later a woman came into view. She was middle-aged, with short grey hair. She walked holding a thick stick with a decorated handle. Her khaki boots crushed pebbles in a way that suggested someone who voted Conservative.

"Middleton! Come, boy!"

The dog, an Irish red setter, ran along the edge of the embankment and sprang down on to the beach.

In the very brief space of time that Tollinger was distracted by this interruption the water-snake vanished.

He stared round anxiously, looking for it. The waste of pebbles was empty, devoid of life.

Tollinger wondered if it had slipped into the sea. He hurriedly stepped out of the water. The foam had slopped over his ankles, drenching his socks. His shoes squelched as he stepped on to dry land. Water fell out through the lace holes.

The woman saw him and waved her stick in greeting.

Tollinger dropped his collection of pebbles and hurried towards him.

"They say there's a storm coming," the woman said, in a gruff, friendly, one-beach-walker-to-another tone. She seemed vaguely familiar. Perhaps she was a minor actress of the type who regularly appeared in bit parts on TV or the movies.

"Yes, very likely," Tollinger replied, his voice a little shaky. He nodded at the sky over beyond the anchored tankers. There, the clouds had boiled up, blotting out the last expanses of blue. The colour of a bruise, they were moving closer. The atmosphere was cloying and heavy.

The woman walked on. Her dog ran past and went along the beach, barking frantically. Tollinger wondered if it had sensed the presence of the water-snake. The dog ran in zig-zags up and down the shoreline, as if in pursuit of an invisible adversary.

Tollinger was not a dog-lover but on this occasion he felt a keen sense of gratitude. This woman and her rust-coloured quadruped had spared him from the snake's unwanted attentions. Once she was past him and had her back turned – the woman was going on north, from where he'd come, in the direction of Kessingland – Tollinger made his way up the beach. He went around the back of the sand embankment, keeping a sharp eye out for the snake. Mercifully, there was no sign of it.

Here, a bridge formed of parallel railway sleepers, crossed the stream, allowing beach walkers to continue. To the west the stream was a narrow ditch which ended below the bridge as a deep, curdled, muddy mass of water. It emerged from a dense plain of sallow reeds which expanded back from the beach for half a mile or so, ending by some woodland. A path had been trodden down and led away into the shoulder-high reed bed, but it was an uninviting prospect. Besides, for all Tollinger knew, the sinister snake had vanished into it. On the beach side the stream, some two metres wide, had cut a gorge. The water was bluish, purified by its passage through shingle.

He crossed the bridge, went round a small headland, and to his delight saw, far away in the distance, the spectral outline of a pier. It meant he now wasn't too far from Southwold. The pier was a dark line to the left of a clutter of houses from which protruded the pale stump of a lighthouse.

Here, the line of cliffs started again, at first only two or three yards high, then slowly rising up, higher and higher, the further south one went.

The beach ahead was deserted.

By now it was mid-afternoon, and it looked like rain. Tollinger felt a new-found sense of freedom. The bizarre encounter with the snake was over and he was on his way. The miniature lake had dropped out of sight, along with the gloomy headland of fallen trees and the woman with her dog. He heard the animal yap once or twice, then heard it no more as the animal and its mistress continued into the distance, out of his sight and hearing.

He walked on for a couple of minutes, breathing deeply, his nerves beginning to settle.

This tranquil mood did not last.

A quick dark triangular shadow flickered along the beach, so quickly that Tollinger at first wondered if it was a spot in his bloodshot eye, abruptly rolling across his vision.

The next instant a massive roaring exploded above him, making him jump.

It was, he realised, the shadow of an RAF jet, screaming down the coast. It was moving so fast the sound of it wrenching apart the atmosphere occurred where the jet no longer was. Tollinger stared up at the reverberating sky. A little speck of silver was vanishing to the south.

As his nerves settled down again, he heard another noise. A kind of scratching noise.

No, not scratching. The sound of something moving very lightly on shingle.

He turned round.

This was much, much worse than the unexpected howling of a jet screaming past low overhead.

The water-snake was back. It was sidling along behind him, its head once more raised high. It was like being attended by a faithful pet.

But those eye slits did not strike Tollinger as being affectionate. Or was he being snakist? After all, a snake cannot help how it looks. Perhaps it was unfair of him to impute hostile intent. His prejudice had been shaped by movies.

It was then that something opened in the snake's blank face – something as small and wrinkled as an anus. What came out of the darkness of this grotesque, widening mouth was not venom but sound. It seemed to spit bolts of sound – little needles of excruciatingly high-pitched squealing which pierced Tollinger's ears and penetrated deep into his brain. His head started singing with pain, vibrating with it. Whole choruses of delicate agony howled inside his eardrums. He winced and clapped his hands to his ears.

The rubbery lips seemed to close and then fold away inside the yellowish scales of the hard, unyielding face. In its toughness the snake's physique appeared to be constructed not out of bone or flesh but something more like plastic.

Tollinger knew that this was a perfunctory demonstration of the creature's *power*. It was letting him know it was a bit more than a mere snake. It was monstrous. It was *a beast*. Probably its DNA went back to the time of the dinosaurs, although somewhere along the line it had been tampered with by Satan.

Tollinger cloudily sensed he was having a panic attack. His brain was getting a little starved of oxygen. His face showed a distinctly blue pallor. He felt like he was drowning. He was gulping and gasping for air, even though he was surrounded by the stuff. Lovely fresh air, the seaside, it was dripping with health-giving ozone.

He turned and ran. He decided to run all the way to Southwold. It was probably only a mile or so. He just needed another dog walker and he'd be safe as houses. The *thing* didn't like dogs, that was obvious.

But he was growing tired. Walking on shingle is hard work, running on it even harder. The pebbles sucked at his sodden shoes, reluctant to let him go.

A band of pain had developed in his chest. Sweat was pouring down his face and trickling into the neck of his shirt.

The horror grew worse.

Tollinger's accelerated speed made no difference to the creature. Far from disappearing far behind him, his exertions seemed to act as an inspiration. Its torso moved like a windscreen wiper on the fastest setting. It swished past him on the beach like a blurred, demented boomerang. Then it jerked sideways and caught him around the shin. It tugged like a wayward muscle. It dragged at him, anchoring him.

Tollinger lost his balance. He stumbled and fell.

He went face down into a mass of small yielding pebbles. They smelled of weed and dampness. They were cold and wet as ice. They stung his cheeks.

The creature was wrapping itself around one of his legs. He lashed out and kicked it off.

Tollinger staggered to his feet.

And then the worst horror of all occurred.

The creature returned to the attack. It slid over his shoe and corkscrewed up his leg, moving very fast.

Before he had even quite registered what was happening it had slid on, over his stomach. It wrapped itself around his chest like a restraint placed upon a mad person. Then, as if pausing for breath, it halted and then, a moment later, moved on.

Suddenly it was resting on Tollinger's shoulder.

Tollinger was close to fainting. The sense of horror and disgust and blind terror was almost overwhelming. His flesh shuddered. His heart thundered. He felt weak and feverish and sick.

The snake's face was just inches from his own. The eyes at close quarters were devilish things, little slender trenches of yellow fire, flecked with bits of gold and shards of dark emerald. The golden dots were restless and animated as maggots thriving in a blackbird's chest cavity.

It was an emperor of abomination. And it stank. This thin, wire-like creature stank of something rancid and decaying. It had fermented in filth, drank on dirt. It had feasted on faeces. It was the living embodiment of vileness. Tollinger sensed it was very old, a hundred years old, older, a thing brewed in darkness. It swayed and seemed to brush its cheek against his. It felt colder than marble – marble coated in slime. Even that slight, momentary contact left an acid spittle burning into his skin.

Tollinger was completely paralysed. All he could do was

sweat and hurt and stare. The beast's neck was a patchwork of ever-changing colours. It had chameleon qualities. And as these perceptions tumbled through his mind like the last defences of a besieged castle, he realised something else.

This monstrous entity was seeking *a host*. It was bored with its little shallow pool on a forsaken windswept beach. It fancied warmer hospitality.

That knowledge made Tollinger sick to the acrid depths of his burning guts. It was enough to make him vomit, were it not that his throat was stretched out and dried-up. The muscles of his neck were rigid and stressed and incapable of action.

Tollinger knew what it was about to do, and in some queer way it seemed to encourage and allow that perception. It allowed it so that he would do exactly what he did do. It greased the way for its final overcoming of his pathetic and puny resistance. The knowledge of what it was about to do – the creature's sinister gift of passing on a brief slice of telepathy – caused him at last to scream.

Tollinger opened his mouth and screamed. He screamed for help, for human assistance. He screamed for a woman with a stout walking stick and a barking dog. But the beach was deserted. The weather had seen to that. Far out at sea, beyond the tankers, lightning flickered. A few moments later came a low slither of thunder. A wall of grey rain could be seen moving slowly inland across a sea dappled with silver.

Tollinger screamed and as he screamed the creature brought its gently swaying head up close to his wide open, taut, straining lips. It was as if it was trying to see inside his mouth. But that was not its ambition. Instead it seemed to position itself and then, without further ado, it launched itself forwards with a convulsive jerk, like a springing cat.

It filled up Tollinger's mouth. It was like a swelling, seething ball composed of compressed writhing tentacles. He felt small hard muscles probing, squeezing, exploring. The snake's presence sealed off his throat and blocked his screams. His eyeballs swelled up with pain and shock. His tongue was in agony, crushed against the floor of his palate.

The snake's head slid around, probing. Then, abruptly, it forced itself down his throat. Its passage scraped its walls, sending out waves of fiery pain. He felt the abomination moving down through the narrow pipes and corridors inside him. The tip of its tail protruded from his mouth like a cigarillo. The tail was hard, wiry, powerful. It was motionless. It made Tollinger choke. He emitted a barely audible gurgling. His muscles convulsed and burned but it was impossible to cough this foulness out.

At the end of the tail was a pair of slender delicate floppy fins, light as cotton, resembling rudimentary wings.

With a sudden flick and jerk it was gone. It followed the rest of that foul thing down his throat. Tollinger gasped and spluttered. He cried out, a low thin squeal of agony. He felt the snake hard inside him, pushing and forcing and worming its passage. He felt it thrusting all the way down to the pit of his hot burning stomach. He seemed to know – to feel – when the tail had followed the rest of the entity to that place. And once it was there Tollinger had the distinct impression of it curling up there. It was at peace, in need of rest. He could feel it there, as if he'd swallowed a length of hosepipe. It filled him up.

And then a great convulsive churning wave of nausea and horror and utter disgust swept over him. Darkness poured across his vision.

He collapsed unconscious on the beach.

4

WHEN HE WOKE it was thick night. A rich, dense, deep, curdled night. The sea sounded very close. Tollinger looked at his watch. Four hours had passed since his encounter with the sea-snake. The beach was in darkness. The tide was coming in.

Tollinger stood and pressed a hand against his stomach. He prodded it, experimentally. He expected to feel movement, but there was none.

He remembered everything before he'd blacked out. He

wondered if it had been a hallucination. He'd taken a range of drugs in his past. Some in the fairly recent past. Even more in the unfair recent past. Maybe this was blowback – a delayed lurid fantasy hatched from some fold of chemically damaged cells.

Sometimes odd memories broke into his mind, strange visionary episodes which seemed like nothing he'd ever truly experienced. In one recent example he was on a main landing, staring over its scrolled iron-gilt balustrade. A big Moorish lantern, hanging at the same level, threw its light on the colourful Persian rugs and brocaded settees in the hall below. When he turned away he saw a massive white pyramid inscribed with hieroglyphics. None of this meant anything to him.

But the snake had seemed awfully real. And he sensed the creature was still inside him, even though his poking and prodding produced no response. He felt a coiled heaviness inside him. A lumpish obstruction. An iron presence with a cool remote-controlled pulse.

But he was still alive – that was something. That was everything. As long as you are alive you have the edge on the dead. They can no longer have the fun you have. They can't enjoy a cool pint on a warm evening, with a view of the marshes and a dozen shelducks. They can't have sex. They can't go to the movies or read a novel. They can't enjoy a good curry or steak and chips.

He needed medical help. He was alive, and that was good, but he was feverish with fear. He needed an X–ray. A medical test would establish if what had happened was more than just a kink in his mind.

His eyes adjusted to the night. The sky was full of stars. But the Milky Way never looked as good as it did in photographs.

The beach was visible through a monochrome haze.

In the distance the green twinkling light from the beacon at the end of the pier perforated a speck of the dark ocean. Tollinger set off in its direction.

He trudged along a narrow strip of shingle with the waves

breaking beside him. The boiling phosphorescence lit the way along the shore. A parallel strip of dull sand showed grey along the foot of the steep cliff. Dark clumps of grass spotted the crumbling cliff-face like symptoms of disease. From time to time a slimy glistening trail of water glowed in a fissure. Tollinger crunched on along the pebbles. He felt tired and washed-out. He wondered if he was sickening for something. His face felt hot and sweaty. His throat felt very sore. His mouth had an unpleasant brackish taste.

The pier seemed to get a little closer.

Tollinger reached a small headland. It loomed darkly, pressing forward.

Here, the cliff dipped down and beyond a heap of topsy-turvy concrete blocks met a sea wall. The smooth wall curled up, like a frozen perfect wave, with a slight lip along its crown.

A row of four groynes comprised of boulders extended into the sea. They were coated with a soft weed. The waves slopped and gurgled around them.

A narrow gap in the long wall provided access to a short flight of steps. Tollinger went up them and emerged on to an expanse of rough, gravel-strewn waste land. Beyond it, at the far north end, a deserted car park was illuminated by streetlights. Tollinger hurried towards it, moving much faster now that he was off the soft sand and the shingle. Reaching the car park, he walked past a long line of striped beach huts. They had cute names which afterwards he struggled unsuccessfully to recall. He could no longer see the sea, but he could hear the waves smashing themselves to pieces on the beach.

At the end of the car park was the entrance to the pier. Although the cream-coloured structure blazed with light, it seemed to be empty. There was no one at the tables in the restaurant. Looped white bulbs swayed on wires. The pier seemed lonely as the *Titanic*, blazing with illumination in the Atlantic's dark immensity.

Tollinger's eyes always brimmed with moisture at the end of that movie, as the dream lovers kiss to the applause of the smiling drowned ones.

Even close up there was no one visible behind the pier's bright plate windows. Below it the ocean boiled around the rusty supports.

Across the road was a hut and the dark rectangle of a Crazy Golf course. The road ran on up the slight slope, the German Ocean on one side, terraced houses on the other. Tollinger set off along this road into the centre of the little town.

Ten minutes later he passed a doorway above which was the name Back To Front Cottage. Shortly afterwards he arrived in the High Street. A fake Victorian hand pump stood slightly off-centre in the triangular town square.

Tollinger walked past The Swan and went a little further up the street. The interior of The Crown looked mostly empty. A couple ate a meal. A solitary man sat at the bar contemplating the galaxies inside a pint of bitter.

Tollinger went between the neo-classical pillars of the stone porch and stepped inside. A smiling young woman in black confirmed they had a room for the night. Tollinger said he'd take it. And your luggage?

"I have none."

She frowned and looked apprehensive but said nothing.

Tollinger didn't feel hungry. That must be the heaviness inside him, he decided. But he knew he should eat something. He ordered a ham sandwich and said he'd eat it in the back bar. It was tiny and deserted. In the corner was some sort of machine, a cross between a beehive and a pump. It was something to do with brewing or shipping. Tollinger didn't care what it was. Heritage machinery had never interested him. Ploughs were for ploughmen. Early automobiles were for dullards. Propellers were for boys. Kettles kept changing shape. Somewhere out there was a kettle museum. And it wasn't just kettles. It was everything. The fountain pen displaced the nib pen, the typewriter displaced handwritten text, the electric typewriter edged out the manual typewriter, the PC with printer rendered the typewriter obsolete, laptops displaced PCs, tablets displaced laptops. The Vortex edged out tablets and smart phones. And so it went on.

But the pen had not entirely disappeared. Rollerball liquid ink devices continued to be sold in newsagents for the benefit of those who still hand-wrote shopping lists, or letters, or notes for future novels.

Tollinger realised he felt feverish and a little odd. The paintings of ships which hung on the wall were all askew. The floor seemed to tip away at an angle. The windows at the back of the bar seemed opaque, twisted. The barman looked at him oddly as he held out another brandy. The barman was now displaying a moustache. Tollinger had a feeling it hadn't been there earlier.

The young woman in black brought him his plate of sandwiches. She set them down in front him. Her smile exposed perfect teeth.

"I asked for ham."

"Oh no, sir. You very definitely asked for cheese."

The bar man joined in. "You did, sir. I heard you say so myself."

Tollinger scowled. "Oh, very well. Forget it. It doesn't matter." He asked for a pint of bitter.

The cheese had been smeared with pickle and wrapped in lettuce. The lettuce was probably saturated in pesticide. It quite possibly harboured a dozing caterpillar. Tollinger knew that he was expected to open it up and check, so he decided to defy expectation. The sandwich slid down, lumpily. Tollinger's throat still hurt. The bitter helped to rid it of the gobbets of food. He left the bar and went upstairs, swaying slightly.

He did not feel good. Good he did not feel. Poorly and hot he was, he felt. His room was at the back, at the back, at the back. There was a small view of a dark drab courtyard. In that space were positioned parked nouns and some wafer-thin outbuildings. Glistening Tollinger closed the curtains. He stripped off his heavy and humid clothes. He splashed some water on his face and then slid into bed.

His brow was burning. He touched his stomach, lightly. He knew it was still there, that thing. He couldn't feel it but he didn't want to wake it up by prodding. It was unquestionably there. His blood told him so. It was tainted in some way. He would have to go to the doctor. He needed medical help. He couldn't go on, bearing this creature like a foetus. He needed an abortion.

He seemed to be awake for a very long time. The town was very quiet, as if everyone else was dead. But somehow, despite the thudding horrific awareness of the abomination inside him, despite what had occurred, he managed, somehow, to fall at last asleep.

Tollinger woke. He lay motionless on his bed. The sheets were soaked. His body was icy cold and coated with sweat.

He was uncertain if he was really awake or inside a dream. Perhaps he was fictitious, in that place where window frames quivered and where a character might perceive the living and the dead as equally ghostly and unreal. What place is that? An annotation might assist. Or an Ibuprofen or two. His head was in turmoil. Had he been asleep? A half-sleep, surely. He remembered waking up, groaning and sighing. He had the shakes. The abomination throbbed within him. He sensed its presence in his blood. He was infected by its foulness. He turned over, repeatedly, trying to find a position in which he might secure sleep. Somehow, his head gripped by violent spasms, he nodded off. Hideous visions unfolded in those deepest recesses of sleep. They seethed and bubbled. Something soft and heavy was lying on his chest, staring at him with yellow eyes.

The bedside clock said it was ate. Ate and a bit. A minute past ate. He dressed, and went down to breakfast, unshaven. The thing inside him was still asleep. He could almost convince himself he'd imagined the whole thing. But he knew he hadn't.

He didn't feel hungry. He ordered orange juice, coffee, and toast with two poached eggs. The eggs made him feel queasy. They looked like little aborted creatures. In the end all he ate was a scrap of toast. As it went down his throat it felt rough and painful.

The waitress told him where the town surgery was.

Tollinger paid his bill and checked out. He walked further up the High Street. He went past Daddylonglegs.

A balding man went by in the opposite direction. He was wearing a blue T-shirt which bore the printed message I AM NOT INSANE. The man said, "Millions of buckets in the soup!" and Tollinger, who decided he had probably misheard, nodded and forced a half smile.

Tollinger turned left at Fat Face. He remembered that Emily, from an earlier draft of his life, liked shopping there.

A pudgy youth with an acned forehead walked by wearing a white T-shirt with a message set out in a gigantic Times Roman font against a scarlet blood-spatter background.

KEEP CALM
AND CARRY ON KILLING ZOMBIES.

The surgery was a low red-brick building like an elongated bungalow. The past tense apt because it's since closed down for good. Before that a cinema was sited there, where George Orwell watched monochrome giant mouths speak American. Tollinger, unaware of this resonance of particles, went inside.

He had to wait at reception while the old woman in front of him talked about her condition. She was taking medication to thin her blood. And she had a heart flutter. And one of her toes did not look at all good. And then the conversation turned to the scarecrow trail, whatever that was. Apparently there was a scarecrow of a fisherman and a whale. The receptionist, a jolly woman with pink cheeks marbled with violet veins, chatted back.

Tollinger fretted at the delay. He had to remind himself he was in Suffolk, where things move at a sluggish, parochial pace. It was as bad as being in Malaysia, Nigeria or Ireland.

At last the old woman was finished, and tottered off to sit in the waiting area with the other dying geriatrics.

The receptionist beamed at him expectantly.

"I'm not registered here," Tollinger said. "But I need to see a doctor urgently. I've swallowed a spoon. I am in great pain."

He'd thought it out. Best not to say he'd been attacked by a mysterious marine snake, which had forced its way inside him. They'd think he was mad. They would subject him to dialogue packed with banal assumptions. He would be patronised. The doctor would produce a dubious smile. Tollinger might find himself sectioned. Then he'd spend the rest of his days like in a movie, shaking the bars in a cell, screaming that there was a snake inside him, with no one taking him seriously.

Plus he was unshaven, which always creates a bad impression.

The receptionist's warmth ebbed.

"We can't see anyone not registered with our practice," she said. "You'll have to go to casualty. The nearest hospitals are in Beccles and Lowestoft."

"I'm in agony," Tollinger said. "I do believe I need to go to hospital. But I don't think I can get there under my own steam."

And in truth, he felt rotten. Luckily, he looked it too. His face was a mask of sweat. He felt as if he was burning up. He surely had a temperature. He swayed a little.

"I feel close to collapse," he affirmed.

Frowning, the woman rose from her stool. "Just a moment. I will talk to someone." She bobbed away and whispered to a woman in a nurse's uniform who was sitting at a desk, writing on a form. Whisper, whisper, whisper. The nurse swivelled her head and scrutinised Tollinger. Whisper, whisper.

The receptionist returned. "If you care to take a seat over there, the nurse will see you. What did you say your name was?"

An odd question, because he hadn't.

"Tollinger. Clifford Tollinger."

"Date of birth?"

"The first of the fourth, eighty-four."

"Surgery?"

"I'm registered with the Polyclinic in Leyton. But since I moved to Suffolk I haven't bothered to find a new doctor."

The receptionist scowled. "You really must do that, you know. You really must." She sniffed. "Now please be seated."

The only available reading matter was a glossy magazine, *Suffolk*. Tollinger learned from it that when off-duty a smart Suffolk estate agent favoured a Bortoni jacket, an Oscar shirt, Tommy Hilfiger chinos, a Robert Charles belt, a Profumo pocket square, and suede brogues. Tollinger felt diminished by this recitation of style. He had only ever heard of Tommy Hilfiger, and this was only because he sometimes read a daily newspaper. Profumo was a name he associated with an ancient British sex scandal. Who the hell was Robert Charles? Who was Bortoni? An Italian, presumably.

"Mr Tollinger!"

The nurse beckoned to him through a pair of electronically operated doors, to her room. He lay down on the bed at her command. Brightly she enquired about the spoon. Tollinger gave her the story he had concocted. A picnic on the beach. A stupid mishap. At first no anxiety, the thought that it would emerge, ahem, naturally. But then, this morning, just an hour ago, *agonising pain*.

Nurse raised his shirt and pushed her hand into his abdomen. She pressed deep into the folds of his belly. Tollinger sensed intestines moving aside at her no-nonsense thrusting.

She reached deep into the pit of his being. Tollinger felt, distinctly, the snake. He knew it was still there, coiled and hard. The nurse's exploratory probe had disturbed it. The creature stirred.

The nurse surely felt it too. She was frowning. She looked perplexed.

She continued to prod and poke. The snake twisted, irritably. Tollinger could feel its wiry loop, its mild uncurling of its rubbery yet granite-hard strength.

The nurse said: "I think I need to get a doctor." Her voice quivered. It was low and edgy. She left the room. In her absence the sea-snake flexed its muscles and did a turn of his solar plexus, like a Jane Austen character in the Assembly Room at Bath. The snake movements were slow and casual. Perhaps it was still waking from a deep sleep.

She returned with a sallow middle-aged man who said his

name was Dr Duck. Had he really said that? It seemed he had. He reached over and pushed his fingers into the pit of Tollinger's stomach.

His reaction was the same as the nurse's. He began frowning. Finally, he looked perplexed. "I think we need to get you into hospital." They left the room. Tollinger stared at a stain on the ceiling. The nurse eventually returned. "An ambulance is on its way," she said. "You can stay here until it arrives."

She looked worried.

5

THEY WANTED to put him on a stretcher but Tollinger felt that his length was about right and so he insisted on walking. It was only once he was inside the ambulance that he agreed to lie down. A woman in a green pantomime costume sat with him on the journey up the A12. She was buoyant with fake good cheer. She asked what brought him to Southwold. Tollinger invented some rubbish about a walking holiday inspired by that arid, bloodless, evasive encyclopaedia of posturing indulgent narcissism, *The Rings of Saturn*. It was a foolish ploy as this simply provoked a fresh round of simplistic interrogation. It was worse than having a trim at the hands of a loquacious hairdresser zealous for the fortunes of Leyton Orient. In the end he closed his eyes to blot out her witless inquisition. He pretended to nod off. Tollinger smiled authentically in his inauthentic sleep, remembering what Pablo Neruda had once written: "Anyone who doesn't read Cortázar is doomed". It was a consoling thought that both his NHS companion and his old hairdresser were among those vast tribes of the damned.

The siren yowled and yowled, so Tollinger knew it was bad. This knowledge delighted him. He knew the snake was not his imagination. It had *really happened.*

At the hospital they insisted on putting him into a wheelchair. He was taken off down a long corridor. A new nurse accompanied him on his journey, while an orderly pushed. The orderly was a black man, the nurse mixed race. They passed through several sets of doors. Finally they turned off into a room with a scanner. It resembled something a dentist might use. The machine was beside a bed, which Tollinger was instructed to lie down on.

The orderly took the wheelchair back into the corridor and waited there. The nurse loitered.

The person operating the scan was a young Asian woman. She asked Tollinger to unbutton his shirt. When he'd done so she rubbed jelly across his stomach. Then she lowered the head of the scanner and pressed it against his skin. It resembled a shower attachment on a ribbed, flexible cord. The machine had a screen, which was turned away. The scanner operator looked at it as she slid the scanner to and fro.

She gasped and frowned. Tollinger knew she was seeing the snake.

The operator beckoned the nurse over and pointed. The nurse gave a little yelp of shock. Her face had turned pale. She said: "I'll call Dr Jones."

The jelly felt cold and unpleasant. But Tollinger did not have to wait long. The doctor arrived quite quickly.

The nurse and the scanner operator pointed at the screen. Stooping to examine it, Dr Jones looked both startled and suspicious. He took charge of the scanner and moved it across Tollinger's stomach. He frowned and shook his head. There was a faint rattling sound but that must have been someone clattering crockery in the ABC commissary. Dr Jones drew back, pursing his lips, the veins in his neck tightening like umbrella struts. A worm wriggled beneath his left eye, pulling the dark pouch closer. The doctor was a thesaurus of nervous mannerisms which supplied a colourful contrast to the banality of his surname. He said in a tremulous whisper: "I need to get Mr Reason. He needs to see this with his own eyes."

Tollinger lay there, saying nothing. He wondered who else's eyes Mr Reason might use. He knew he didn't need to ask what their conversation meant. These medical professionals were seeing what was really there, coiled inside him like a length of rubber.

Mr Reason was a consultant Gastroenterologist. He was slender, with silvery-grey hair. He had a quiet, authoritative manner.

Dr Jones pointed at the screen. "You see what I mean," he said in a low, shaky voice. The worm was still there, tugging excitedly at his eye.

The consultant took one look at the screen and then turned and asked everyone to leave. When they'd gone he said to Tollinger: "Do you have any idea what is inside you?"

Tollinger said: "It's some kind of living creature, isn't it?"

He told the consultant, very briefly, what had occurred on the beach.

Mr Reason listened without interrupting. He looked thoughtful. He said: "You are going to need specialist surgery, urgently. I shall take steps to see that you get it. We can't do it at this hospital, however. I am going to prescribe you some Diazepam to relax you. I also suggest you say nothing to any of the staff here at this hospital. I'm afraid this matter is rather outside their everyday experience."

The orderly came back into the room with the wheelchair. Tollinger was taken away. The man wheeled him off down a different corridor, through more doors, to deposit him another room. This one contained nothing but easy chairs, a difficult novel, a nurse, some magazines, yesterday's *Metro* and a water machine. A previous patient had either forgotten or finished with their paperback copy of a Modern Classic which lay on a chair beside the *Metro*. Tollinger glanced at the book's introduction. It asserted that readers of the book "marvel at the accuracy and miasmic clarity of the evocations but wrestle with the narrative strategies".

The new nurse was there to wait with him – an extra without a speaking part, whose function was to stand by him, looking grave yet supportive. Tollinger didn't even notice the gender of this uniformed figure, let alone the type of hair or the colour of

43

the eyes. Another nurse soon arrived – a buoyant, beaming blue-eyed blonde – with those all-important pills. She was permitted two words: "Take these."

Tollinger swallowed them and within minutes felt a warm, pleasant sensation spread through his body. The sensual pleasure supplied by these chemical stimulants merged with the agreeable feeling of being someone important, who was at the centre of attention, being cared for by trained medical professionals who took his condition seriously.

Mr Reason reappeared, together with the black orderly and the wheelchair. Once more Tollinger was wheeled away down corridors and through twin doors. This time his destination was the back of the hospital. There was an overflow staff car park there, almost empty at this time of day. It lay before them as they came out of the last doorway.

They waited by some large grey waste containers which were placed against the rear wall of the hospital. The consultant looked sombre. He said nothing. The sky was cloudy and overcast. Out of it, almost at once, came a distant whirring. The sound grew louder. Soon the chopper was above them, circling. The pilot chose a suitable space in the car park and the big dark machine descended. Through the warmth and euphoria of his flesh Tollinger felt the snake inside him stir. The creature sensed there was trouble ahead.

Tollinger felt both feverish and elated. Although no one had told him – had they? – he knew the helicopter was for him. The monster inside him had gifted him with importance. There was an urgency about his condition. Experts were interested in him. Top professionals wished to probe. Manicured, fragrant hands would don surgical gloves, just for him.

He was surprised, though, that the helicopter was a military one. Its livery was khaki. As it settled on the ashphalt surface the rotors whipped up a thin cloud of brown dust and blasted scraps of litter away from its descending abdomen.

A pair of soldiers wearing khaki jumped out and came towards them. The consultant pointed: "This is my patient, Mr Tollinger. Goodbye, Mr Tollinger."

The soldiers helped him from the wheelchair and lifted him up into the chopper. The interior was a dark metallic oval. Its structure was hard and skeletal. It was like getting inside a gigantic model of a dragonfly.

Tollinger was gently supported to a chair at the rear and strapped in. Ridges like thin shelves ran around the walls, just above his head.

Apart from the two soldiers who'd helped him aboard the only others present were the helmeted pilot and co-pilot. Once he was aboard one of the soldiers slid the door closed and the chopper's rotor blades screamed faster and faster. The machine tilted forward, then rose into the air. The simulation was fantastically convincing.

The helicopter soared up over the hospital and turned south, towards Lowestoft. The town came into view almost at once. The pilot steered his machine towards the sea and the town's little stubby lighthouse passed by below.

They followed a course which ran parallel to the shore. From up here the Gulliver wind turbine looked like a little garden ornament. Tiny cars moved in lines along strips of road like an army of slow beetles. A band of green fields was almost at once blighted by a star-shaped infection of housing. Then more fields and patches of woodland slid by.

Southwold Pier passed below them, twinned with the stiff protruding mouth of the River Blyth.

Marshland, with glittering ditches. Swathes of dark, dense forest.

The great white dome of Sizewell B looked tranquil in the late afternoon light. A few miles beyond it, rising out of woodland, stood the dream-like House in the Clouds. The planet's surface was bronzed and benign.

On the beach people standing by the giant scallop sculpture stared up. The helicopter's shadow flashed over them. A pair of children waved.

Beyond the next town a wide brown river came out of the interior, nudged a bank of shingle, and, obstructed, rolled away south. The landscape below was a desolation of mud and estuary and shingle. The adjacent land looked brown and desolate. It might have been a barren stretch of Africa.

The embankments and estuaries below were eroded by tributary streams. Their shapes were distinctly snake-like. Seeing them Tollinger felt sick.

Perhaps the pills were wearing off.

Perhaps the creature inside him was waking up. Tollinger sensed it stirring uneasily in his stomach. It knew something was up. Tollinger wondered if it was capable of feeling fear. He supposed so.

The noise of the engine increased in pitch as the helicopter began to descend.

They landed and the two soldiers helped Tollinger out. He stood on the ground, swaying. His fever had returned. The snake was moving inside him. He could feel its head as it circled his hot wet stomach lining. Perhaps it was searching for the exit. The creature had had a comfy night's accommodation and now it wanted to be on its way. Its body felt as if it was composed of wire and rubber. Tough but a little abrasive, as if ridged. That would be its scales, Tollinger supposed.

The ground he was standing on was cracked. Star-shaped green weeds sprouted from the fissures. The place they were in might have been a deserted aerodrome. It was derelict. There was a hut with broken windows, near which lay obscure scraps of rusting machinery. In the distance was a line of tall, slender towers. They had some resemblance to pylons, but they were placed close together and there were no wires. Near them stood a massive windowless building which looked like a power plant. It must have been five or six storeys high. Hard to tell when there were no windows.

Tollinger had assumed he was being taken to another hospital. Now he felt a chill of fear. Why had they brought him to this strange, lonely place? Was he about to be executed? Would they throw his body in the sea? He'd seen that movie *The Ghost*. He knew what happened when you disturbed the status quo. Found drowned, Clifford Tollinger. *Mr Tollinger is believed to have been trapped by the tide while walking south of Kessingland. A spokesman for the coastguard service warned that...*

The soldiers took hold of his arms and led him towards a green mound resembling a tumulus.

Behind them came a rising whine and a blast of dust as the helicopter took off.

The tumulus was like Sutton Hoo, only steeper, taller, bigger. But of course, it was merely an old military bunker, protected by earth. It had a small porch flanked by concrete buttresses, between which was a metal door. One of the soldiers unlocked the door and they stepped inside.

When the door was closed they stood for a few moments in pitch blackness. Then strip lighting along the walls flickered into life. Tollinger saw that they were standing at one end of an empty hangar. It was a bleak, chilly place. The curved ceiling was made of corrugated metal. It was like a kind of tomb.

Their footsteps echoed as the soldiers led him to the end. Tollinger noticed that there were dark CCTV blisters dotted about the ceiling.

At the end they went through another locked door. On the far side was a much smaller chamber. It was square, with a door set into one wall. Here there were two more CCTV blisters. The tall soldier pressed a button in the wall and the door slid sideways. It was, Tollinger realised with a start of surprise, an elevator. This was just like the movies!

The control panel inside had a series of brushed-steel buttons. The soldier pressed LG and the door softly closed. Inside the elevator it was just like being in one in a department store, but without the mirrors on the walls.

Tollinger's stomach contracted as they dropped deeper underground. He felt the snake jerk in surprise and then coil itself at the base of his gut, in a defensive posture. The creature was apprehensive. Its anxiety spread across his nervous system, making him nervous too.

Tollinger and his escort stepped out into a bright, cool, air-conditioned room. A woman in khaki camouflage overalls smiled at them from behind a turquoise desk. She had a wide triangular face. Her irises were bright discs of polished crystal.

The soldiers saluted. "Mr Tollinger, ma'am."

She saluted back. Her tongue made a ticking sound when she spoke.

Tollinger would have liked to seize her in his arms and greedily kiss her on the mouth. He would have liked her to lie passive in his embrace before returning his kiss with a fervour equal to his own. Afterwards he would ask her about the ticking noise. But he did nothing.

She smiled at him. "Welcome to the island, Mr Tollinger. Dr Brooke is expecting you. This way please."

She opened a thick metal door behind her and led the way down a bright, clean corridor lit by fluorescent strips. From grilles in the ceiling could be heard the sound of air-conditioning. After passing a series of numbered doors they came to the one marked 14.

Dr Brooke's office was minimalist in style – a chair, a desk, a flatscreen monitor, a slender filing cabinet. Brooke himself was angular, slender, with a reddish face severely marked by acne.

"How are you feeling, Mr Tollinger?"

"Not A1."

"Quite so. Tell me, do you ever wake and feel as long as a galaxy?"

"Never."

"Does the name Rebecca Cune mean anything?"

"It does not."

"Are the tunnels under Grand Central Station the colour of coral, caramel or cobalt?"

"Viridian."

Dr Brooke laid down his pen and stopped ticking boxes. "Why didn't you answer the question?" The gravity of his voice was tinctured with disappointment.

"I did. Your question reminded me of a moment in a movie I once saw. The question concerned the colour of a woman's eyes." Tollinger's wry smile was barely returned. He took a breath, and then another, and then another one after that.

The doctor slowly shook his head. He gave Tollinger a dark look. He said fiercely, "Well I've seen the scan results. They emailed them to me from the hospital while you were flying down here. We shall operate at once. We need to get this thing out of you A.S.A.P."

"But why here? What is this place?"

"You are in a military hospital. We mostly specialise in battlefield injuries. But we have expertise in other areas. Chemical and biological warfare. Cryomorphic trauma. Latent robot insertion negativities. Residual penetration malformation seeding. I'm afraid the terminology may well seem a little abstruse to a layman such as yourself. But as I'm sure you appreciate all professions develop a specialised vocabulary. Here we work at the very edge of the new battlefield technology. Some of it is inspired by terrorist outcomes, of course. Mostly they are just brutes with a belief but a handful are exceptionally smart. Personally I would never denigrate someone with a doctorate in chemistry, physics or biology."

He paused and looked thoughtful. With a dry, laconic smile he added, "Some of it may come from another place entirely."

"What place is that?" said Tollinger thickly.

"That would be entirely speculative. As of this moment in time our primary and most urgent objective is extraction. Once that is accomplished we can pursue the question of origin. Now please roll up your sleeve."

Tollinger, still a little fuddled by pills and a high temperature, did as he was asked. Dr Brooke injected him with something and at once he felt relaxed and soothed.

"Strange place, this. Are we on an island? It looked like an island from the air."

"It's a sort of island, yes. Now we're all going to go off to the theatre."

Tollinger blinked. "To see what? *The Tempest*, I hope."

Dr Brooke smiled coldly. He did not answer.

Soon Tollinger was lying on a gurney rolling along a long white corridor which smelled of disinfectant. He stared up at the humming silver grey grilles on the ceiling. He remembered the Peter Greenaway adaptation, the books going into the sea. And that movie which flaunts the numbers one to one hundred.

Tollinger was being helped out of his clothes. His slack, lifeless penis seemed unusually small. The harsh light gave it the blotchy yellowish colour of an autumn leaf. A pair of loose white cotton shorts were slipped over his exposed groin. Tollinger lay on the operating theatre table and a woman wearing surgical overalls greased his chest with jelly. Disturbingly, her irises were a golden yellow. Next she pressed electrodes against his skin. He knew this was in case they needed to resuscitate him. He would have liked someone there he knew, someone who would put a comforting arm around his shoulders.

The snake seemed to sense these preparations. It began to flex its muscles, moving restlessly around Tollinger's stomach. It pressed against his stomach lining. He saw a lump suddenly appear near his belly button and knew it was the snake's head, rising up inside him, probing. It knew that matters were racing towards a conclusion. It perceived the threat to it in that place.

The operating theatre looked just like the ones he'd seen in movies. Huge discs of light blazed down from the ceiling. In the background stood metallic trolleys, with silver equipment lying on them.

Masked people in surgical costumes surrounded Tollinger. They might have been actors or they might have been real.

A nurse loomed forwards with a hypodermic needle. "This is to put you to sleep," she said. She had skinny Emily's green eyes. She even sounded like Emily.

"I want you to count to ten," Emily said, as she withdrew the needle. Her breath smelled of peppermint.

Tollinger smiled. Easy-peasy! "One. Two. Threeee. Furrr. Ffffff..."

Oblivion.

6

TOLLINGER WOKE.

A bright light dazzled him. He moved slightly and felt a sharp searing wrench of agony. The pain was savagely acute, in his lower abdomen. His right hand moved to where the flesh-fire was. He probed the spot with his forefinger. Its tip came into contact with something greasy and he pulled it back. The jelly from the electrodes, he supposed. He felt groggy. The etymology from grog, he guessed. Pissed sailors. A Tollinger had served under Nelson, family tradition said. On the *Victory* itself.

Tollinger turned his face away from the fierce, painful brightness which poured down at him from above. With a shock of surprise he saw that he was still lying on the table in the operating theatre. The electrodes were still planted on his chest. They looked like a strange dark variety of mushroom.There was another surprise: the room was empty. Machines winked and glowed but no one attended to them.

He looked at his finger and realised it was dabbled with blood. *Where was everybody?*

He was still wearing the white shorts, but they were spotted with blood. Tollinger went back with his hand to the source of the pain. His finger encountered a sticky, slurpy mass. He pushed it gently into the heart of the soup.

To his horror his entire fist slid instantly into the hole. Tollinger felt his fist inside himself. It seemed to float in slop, nudged by hot wet soft shapes. With a gasp of disgust he jerked it out again. His hand was wet with shining blood, up to the wrist.

He fainted.

Tollinger woke.

A bright light tormented his eyes. His eyelids quivered and closed.

He moved slightly and felt a sharp searing stab of pain. The pain was every bit as intense as earlier, and still rooted in his lower abdomen.

He remembered everything and glanced down at his hand. It was still bright red.

Where in hell is everyone? he thought.

It was like he'd been abandoned mid-operation. The surgeons and nurses had gone.

This is surely a gross breach of medical procedure, he thought angrily. *I shall complain about this.*

He moaned, feeling weak and vulnerable and abandoned.

He had no idea what time it was.

Tollinger twisted his head sideways. At least that didn't hurt, the oval lump balanced on top of his spinal column. The pain was all in his abdomen. In the great fucking hole they'd made there.

He knew they'd done it. They'd successfully extracted it. The snake was gone. He knew that for an instinctual fact. It had gone to some other place. Maybe it was dead. Maybe they'd plucked it out with giant tweezers and then poured fire over it. That's what they would have done in a movie. Fried it to a crisp. He no longer sensed its brain inside him. No more telepathy. No more cerebral bleed. The critter had quit.

But did they have to be so clumsy? They'd made a mess down there. Left him wide open and ragged. Christ knows what germs were feasting on his open wound. Microbes. Billions of them. If he wasn't already dying he was, at the very least, seriously injured.

Had it gone wrong, the op? Was that why there was no one here? Why he'd been apparently abandoned?

Had the snake had *an adverse reaction* to being dug out of Tollinger's stomach? Had it gone crazy?

Tollinger twisted his head sideways. He scanned the empty operating theatre. He saw, for the first time, blood on the floor. He doubted it was his own because it was over by the double doors through which he'd been brought in. A thick trail of blood which vanished under the rubber seal.

His mind raced. Tollinger noticed a trolley loaded with

equipment. Among the plastic jars and the boxes was a big thick roll of cotton wool. That would do, in the first instance.

First, he removed the electrodes. It was agony. Each one resisted his efforts. His shaking fingers kept slipping on the edges. Getting an electrode off required a firm grip and a sudden wrenching movement, which transmitted pain like burning acid through his guts. By the time he'd taken the last one off he was drenched in sweat and drained of energy. He lay back on the table and rested. His mind began to wander and drift. A woman's voice whispered to him. "As far as we know there is no better part of Mars to which we might attempt to escape." She tucked a strand of dark hair under her headscarf and smiled down at him. "It's a lovely dream," she said. "But I'm afraid it can never be more than that." As there seemed to be no more to be said on the matter for the time being, they talked for a while on other subjects. Malcolm Lowry as a correspondent. The letter he wrote from 595 W. 19th Avenue on 24 April 1940, remarking *I have written what I believe to be a really good novel during these last few months – there are three others too, as yet unsold.* The merits of a novel containing the lines *You just go dead inside and everything is easy. You just get dead like most people are most of the time.*

Tollinger was close to falling asleep. He forced himself to stay conscious. He began moving his legs round. He couldn't roll off the operating table, not the easy way, on his stomach. Lying face down was a no-no. He felt if he turned over his intestines would come spilling out. He couldn't risk a spillage. No, he had to get off the table while lying on his back.

The only way to accomplish this was to slide sideways until he was able to lower one leg on to the floor.

Wriggle, wriggle.

The pain rippled through him with every slight shift of his torso. His face was cold with sweat.

Eventually his bare foot touched the hard icy floor. It seemed to be made of linoleum or some other synthetic material. He dragged his other foot to the edge of the table and let it drop. When he twisted his body round and slipped off the table an extra-large pulse of agony bored through him. Tollinger grunted with shock. His whole body was trembling. He felt very weak and very unwell. But at least the snake was out of him.

He stood there for a while, leaning against the table. A slow ooze of gore began to seep downward from the gash in his abdomen.

When he was ready, he tottered towards the trolley.

He managed to get there without collapsing. Feverishly he snatched up the roll of cotton wool. He tore at it, ripping away the paper wrapping. At once the cotton wool went rolling away, unspooling. Clutching one end, Tollinger was unperturbed. There were about five metres of the stuff, as wide as a paperback. He pulled it back towards himself and wrapped it around his waist, covering the bloody ragged hole. The first coating of cotton wool soaked up blood and began to disintegrate. Tollinger quickly buried it under another length, and then wrapped another. He went on until the roll was used up. He made a crude knot in the soft fluffy material, then returned to the trolley. It had on it a roll of sticking plaster of the same industrial dimensions as the cotton wool. A pair of scissors lay beside it.

Tollinger cut several lengths of plaster. He wrapped them over the bands of cotton wool until they were completely concealed.

He leaned against the wall, breathing heavily. Pain still rippled out from the crater in his abdomen. Every movement of his lungs started a new shiver of suffering.

He scrutinised the trolley. There were white bottles at the back. When he had acquired the strength he lurched back and examined them. Most were labelled with the names of medication he'd never heard of. One said simply: LIQUID MORPHINE.

Tollinger struggled with the plastic screw cap for a while, grunting and wincing. Finally it twisted off. He raised the neck of the bottle to his lips and took a gulp.

The liquid burned through him like whisky. Warmth radiated

through his body, followed by a surge of good feeling. His spirits lifted, He felt almost exhilarated. The morphine numbed the pain and gave him strength.

He pushed open the twin doors of the operating theatre. The smear of blood below the doors inside the theatre continued outside. It went along a corridor an under the next door. Instead of following its trail, Tollinger opened each of the four doors in the corridor. One contained surgical tools. One contained lockers and oxygen cylinders. One contained cleaning equipment. One contained new surgical gowns hanging from hooks.

Since he was dressed only in white shorts, Tollinger took down a gown and slipped it around himself. Then, still holding the morphine bottle, he slowly followed the blood trail through the deserted underground hospital.

From time to time he shouted "Hello! Is there anybody there?" His words fell into the silence and were not answered. Everyone had gone, leaving him in the operating theatre, bloody and alone.

There was some evidence of haste. In one room a bottle had been dropped. A pool of dark blue liquid was surrounded by shattered glass.

A woman's black leather shoe lay half-way down a corridor.

Someone had dropped a laptop. It had flipped open, exposing a fractured and fuzzy monitor.

Tollinger came to a room which was obviously his recovery room. It had a bed, a table, a drip tube dangling from a support. On a metal chair was a neat pile of his clothing. Beside it was his rucksack. His watch was there, too. The time was eleven o'clock. Morning or night? Down here it was impossible to tell.

Tollinger took a swig of morphine and got dressed. He slipped the rucksack on.

The trail of blood was like a red guidance line to the way out. He followed it down silent lit corridors to the elevator shaft.

When the doors opened Tollinger saw that there was another woman's shoe lying there. But this one was green.

He emerged in the place where he had first descended, and it was cold.

The blood trail ended. Tollinger made his way out of this place through unlocked doors. Finally he stepped through a door and saw he had arrived back at the empty hangar with the ceiling made of corrugated metal.

The place stank. There was a strong smell of urine. There were dark stains on the walls. The sour reek combined with the stench of voided bowels. There was what looked like filth in the shadows of one corner.

The door was open at the far end, and grey light spilled in. Fighting back great walloping surges of nausea, Tollinger staggered towards it.

Clouds scudded across an overcast sky. A few flakes of ash danced past his face. He realised this was snow.

Beside an object resembling a pulley lay a broken oar, slightly burned along its blade. Tollinger stepped over it and walked towards the spot where the chopper had landed. His wristwatch indicated it would soon be noon.

This was a derelict place. It was littered with the remains of abandoned activity. Scraps of broken machinery lay scattered across long strips of ancient tarmac which resembled runways.

A cold wind poured in from the German Ocean. It pushed against the green weeds which thrived in the ground's many fissures. With an iron crash the door blew shut behind Tollinger. He had a sudden odd feeling that if he tried to return to the underground complex he would find that the door was now locked.

Instead, he headed south, picking his way past the burnt umber carcases of dead machines. The wind whistled among the rusted shreds but Tollinger didn't recognise any of the tunes. He noticed that the snowflakes had stopped.

The pain was returning and walking was an effort. Tollinger took another swig of morphine and the pain melted. He felt good. Buoyant even. The snake was gone. Gone from his body and gone from the neighbourhood. He felt unafraid. Somehow he just knew for sure it wasn't close anymore.

A supermarket's silver cart lay on its side by the hut.

Tollinger's legs felt weak. An idea formed way down in the murk of his mind. First he lifted up the cart. He set it straight. He checked that its wheels still functioned. They did. Next he went back and picked up the oar. He returned to the cart. He lay the oar across it. Then he climbed in. He sat down with his back to the handle. Taking the oar, he began to punt himself along the ground.

Slowly, he rolled himself towards the line of slim, pylon-high towers. They consisted simply of cross-hatched struts. Obviously they were some sort of radio aerial. The big windowless building which looked like a power plant loomed over him as he rolled closer and closer. The blacktop had been freshened up here and the cart ran smoothly (though it squeaked). There was no sign of life in the big building. It didn't look derelict in the way that the rest of this area did, but there was no evidence of any human presence. There were some metal doors. Tollinger punted over to them and tried the handles. The doors were all locked.

He left the towers and the big building behind and travelled on.

He came to a lush zone of marshland dissected by ditches and full of reed banks. The path sank down until the reeds rose up all around him. Here, Tollinger had to abandon his trolley. The path was miry and half overgrown with weed. He used the section of oar as a walking stuck and slithered onward. It took him twenty minutes to get through this belt of swamp. Once he frightened some geese, which erupted noisily out of the yellowish vegetation and shot away inland.

He emerged, moaning slightly as spasms of pain burned in his stomach. Now he was walking south, across a plain of shingle dotted with small tufts of wiry grass and thistles. In the far distance, where the sky was brighter, stood a red and white striped lighthouse. Perhaps it was as derelict as everything else: no light seemed to flash from it.

He limped on, in the direction of a bridge.

When at last he reached the bridge he saw that his path joined a rough carriageway which bore the imprint of vehicle tyres. In one direction it headed off towards the faraway lighthouse. In the other it led off across the bridge towards what looked like a refugee settlement. Scores of brown wooden huts stretched as far as he could see.

There was no sign of movement or life among the huts.

Tollinger crossed the bridge. Below it, a narrow soupy river flowed sluggishly between banks of mud. A semi-submerged object which resembled the letter "A" protruded above the surface. Nearby were the letters "C", "B" and "K". Alphabet soup.

He walked on. When he reached the rows of huts he saw that they were derelict. Smashed windows, rags of curtain, open doors exposing empty interiors. One, adjacent to the rough road, was in better shape. Its frosted glass windows were uncracked. On the padlocked door was a sign: MUSEUM OF LO.

Of what? he wondered.

High board fences creaked and quivered. Some of the panels had blown down. Through the gaps could be seen a plain of weed-seamed shingle, stretching away to the ocean.

Curls of barbed wire ran off sideways like steel hedgerows. Some were folded up into tangled bushes of spikes.

Tollinger walked on, pausing every few minutes to rest on his oar-stick. He felt very tired. The ground he was on now seemed to emit a faint radiance. It seemed to intensify. A sheet of light abruptly washed across him, like a stray lightning flash. He shut his eyes, and a scarlet grid throbbed on a wide screen.

When he opened them the radiance was gone.

He didn't see the dog approach. Suddenly it was there, trotting alongside him, its tongue hanging out. It looked like a mongrel – a mundane creature with a short coat of black and white hair, rather prominent ribs, and an average dog-type head. It lacked the coiffured elegance of a pampered poodle or the stolid, scowling, waddling authority of a bulldog. It accompanied him as if Tollinger was its master and they were out for a quiet stroll together.

"So where did you come from, then?" Tollinger said.

The dog looked up at him with anxious, pleading eyes. It wagged its tail hopefully.

Tollinger kneeled and the dog started to lick him appreciatively. He patted its head and the tail wagged furiously. Then, with a cry of disgust, Tollinger started back. He realised the dog was licking at a trickle of blood which had leaked through his shirt. He pushed the animal away and stood up.

"Go away!" he shouted.

The animal retreated a yard or so and continued wagging its tail.

Tollinger walked on, the dog following.

It was starting to snow again. Harsh dark flakes by the hundred, falling all around him, whitening as they settled on the ground. But no sooner had they fallen to earth than they melted away. They polished shingle and the grass and left wet gleaming surfaces.

In time he reached the pier.

The uneven road consisted of compacted mud and gravel. It wandered through the huts, then sank into another reed bed. It came through the reeds and emerged beside a muddy estuary. There were three or four hundred yards of water and on the far side, the mainland. Tollinger glanced at his watch and realised it was later than he'd imagined. Dusk was forming around the landscape, blurring its sharpness. The mainland was a smooth, fuzzy mass of browns and greens. Marshland, with no sign of human habitation.

Tollinger realised he must have reached the western side of the island.

When he looked back he saw that the dog had gone. So had the snow.

He followed the rough uneven road beside the estuary until it terminated at a pier.

The pier was a simple structure of wooden boards resting on

tall supports rooted in the mud. It protruded out into the darkening estuary for twenty yards or so. The water there was black. A single star burned brightly, low in the sky.

There was a big iron mushroom on this pier, used to tie boats. Tollinger tried to remember the word for it. Stanchion? It didn't matter. He sat down on it and waited.

Everything became slowly darker and darker.

7

EMILY'S LIPS split apart. Scarlet and cracked, they mouthed words. Her language was harsh. Her words were dark and tough. She'd worked them, these words, to a rehearsed smoothness. They rolled out below her clammy eyes. Eyes as cold as a cavern wall inside the Appalachians. Later on she'd go for good and then he'd truly know they could never be as one again.

She said it was best he left.

Tollinger agreed. They'd been happy together but now the joy was gone. Matters had solidified. Their days had become familiar and hard. The original fire was long extinguished.

The bedroom window is steamed up. Emily rubs a hole in the fog. They both knew from the start something was coming to an end. Tollinger watches the movement of her denim-cupped cheeks. The moment their lips first touched their flesh began to shrink. Her small firm breasts lost a tiny fraction of an inch as he touched her nipples. As he shuddered inside her his penis was already beginning to erode. My love, my darling, he gasped, unaware of the shrinkage in his tongue. His lips quivered. Language was cracking in the heat. Several semi-colons became detached and rolled away under the bed. Tollinger cannot forget that hot summer.

He distinctly remembers a pair of linked balloons restlessly blundering around the flowerbed in the garden.

And the trees along the avenue, stunted and thin. The sparrows stamping in the dust. *What happened to the sparrows?* he wondered.

"Where are they?" Dylan Thomas was reputed to have cried out, mysteriously, before he slipped away into death.

One of the balloons was green, the other red. The future has been cancelled, skinny Emily thinly whispers. Tollinger is at first reluctant to admit reality. Reality has a cheap, tinny ring. In the background Bob Dylan is singing "Every Grain of Sand", the recording with a barking dog. Tollinger hands Emily a thumbnail sketch of a blueprint. The future. A house on a cliff, with a fine view. An immaculate kitchen-diner. A leather sofa. She flushes it away. The muscles of his face are alive, distorting his features. Now they are both shrinking fast, very noticeably. Emily is soon barely as tall as a bucket. He himself, sprawled and flat on his face, is little longer than a tennis racket. In the far distance an ice-cream van is playing The Sailor's Hornpipe. Before the end of the melody he is just a few inches tall and getting smaller. The recording ends. It takes months for him to drag himself across the carpet's dust boulders and get as far as the front door. He slips under it. Goodbye, Emily says, her eyes brimming. Have a good life. Yes. And you.

It is only once outside the building that his shrinkage stops and he begins to grow back to normal size again. He is shaking all over. For a while he feels delirious and light-headed but in the end he comes back to earth. He whistles the theme to the old Peter Sellers film *Tom Thumb*. He is starting to feel better already.

After an ending like this, Tollinger thought, you either sink or you float. He chose to float. He wanted the pattern of his life broken. He'd see where the current took him. Not that his drift was as passive or original as he maybe believed. Character and destination are shaped by forces not necessarily visible or understood. There are strange laws of motion. Plus, in a sequence of fictions, the foundations and walls are frequently concealed. Authority has a smooth, commanding tongue and the blue sky masks everything beyond it. The camera crew, the equipment, is all outside the shining, perfect frame. Sprockets no longer catch or tear, the image never jams, turns amber, and explodes. Digitalisation has done for all that. Besides, who is saying this, anyway? Not Tollinger, surely.

Remember Stahr. A name which merges *stare* and *star*.

If he was going to die soon, like the two doctors said, he wanted to stop being Stahr for a while. Wrote F. Scott Fitzgerald, who would shortly die.

A thought incubated inside Tollinger's drowsy mind: you need night and dark to see the stars.

And now, lo! The stars are beginning to switch on, one by one. Over there, the Dog Star, surely... Yes. Dog days are here again. Dog years. Doggedly, he endured. Doggedly, he waited to see what would happen next.

Night wraps its cool velvet itself around Tollinger. His lungs inhale a cold frosty sharpness. Up there, across the firmament, the bright company accumulates, like a growing army of dead souls. The jewels of Orion's Belt, the sparkling outline of the Dragon. The blur of the Pleiades. Arcturus, Altair, Centauri... The Tannhauser Gate.

Next an abrupt enigmatic blinding incandescence, a huge rushing splash of light, a sheet of perplexing whiteness, expanding.

Close your eyes, then open them again. Eyes wide. It's a warm, quiet night. But not for long. A distant remote mosquito's whining transforms itself into the unmistakeable sound of an outboard motor. It sounds like a saw, cutting through the turmoil inside him.

The inky water is hatching a boat, Tollinger thinks. He mops at his wet forehead. He needs tablets, he is certain of it. Did he have any? He can't remember. Now he's feverish again. His fever is seamed with rippling bands of nausea. A choking sensation pinches his throat. He feels weak and numb.

The boat parts the darkness with a creamy bow wave. The helmsman shines a flashlight at him.

A probing incandescence.

"Have no fear! Help is at hand! Missed the last ferry, did we?

Not to worry. Happens all the time."

Tollinger stared at the man, who was stretching out his hand.

"Come on! Haven't got all day." His hand was big and firm and dry.

Tollinger climbed down into the boat.

"Over there."

The boatman was a large, overweight man with a Father Christmas beard and an ebullient manner. His skin was florid. He was wearing a dark cloak, like Dracula.

The boatman waved a podgy finger.

"Naughty, naughty! You should pay more attention to the timetable."

Tollinger felt like vomiting. Each rock of the vessel sent spasms cascading down the hot narrow twists of his gut.

"Not to worry. We'll have you back on the mainland in no time. Reunite you with your loved ones, and all that, what?"

The man laughed a laugh that was structured as three short quick and connected laughs. Hahaha!

Tollinger sat facing the helmsman. He stared past him at the phosphorescence which the bow wave created in the dark water. It seemed to mirror the sky above, which was filled with bands of sparkling stars. A twinge of pain in his stomach brought him back from outer space.

The man was shouting now, trying to make himself heard over the noise of the throbbing outboard. "Wife worried. Children upset. Happens all the time. Not to worry! Back to the family in two ticks!"

The boat carved the night. They might have been in the middle of the Atlantic. Nothing visible but foam and galaxies.

The helmsman's mobile phone piped a few bars from Celine Dion's disaster classic.

"Yes. Almost certainly. Couldn't be anyone else. Okey-dokey. Yes. Quite so. Yes. In a jiffy. Okey-dokey. *Ciao.*"

When he'd put his phone away he looked sombrely across at Tollinger and said: "Not long now. Any minute, in fact."

Tollinger turned round and was surprised to see that the boat had almost reached a brightly lit landing place. It formed part of a small harbour. On a short promontory to the right of the harbour wall a yellow crane stood beside a large white cabin cruiser which rested on wooden supports. To the rear the pale outline of more boats showed.

Behind the harbour a street extended up a gentle slope. The street was lined with buildings. In the darkness beyond, scattered lighted windows glowed.

The tide was high, so it was easy disembarking. Tollinger steadied himself and stepped on to the quayside.

To his surprise the boat moved away again, the helmsman giving him a brief wave of farewell.

Tollinger walked across the quay, the palm of his right hand pressed against his stomach. To his horror it felt wet there. When he looked at his palm it was bright with blood.

His clothes were sodden there. The wound must have opened up again. Oddly, he felt no pain, just a dull nausea.

Six figures came out of the darkness in front of him. They seemed to be wearing navy-blue uniforms.

"Mr Tollinger?"

He nodded. "That's me," he said thickly.

The lead uniform, a man in his thirties with a square jaw and a grim expression, came closer. He scrutinised Tollinger in the lamplight. He said: "You don't look too good." (Irony from square-jaw grim-expression!)

"I'm bleeding. Quite badly, I think."

The man clicked his fingers and a white vehicle cruised out from behind the crane. AMBULANCE.

"Don't worry. We'll soon get you sorted out, Mr Tollinger."

They helped him into the ambulance and he lay down.

Two of the uniformed men climbed in and sat alongside him. They laid towelling across the blood oozing from his stomach. Tollinger noticed they had cloth badges sewn to the shoulders of their uniforms.

MERRIVALE HOSPITAL.

It didn't seem to take too long to get to where they were going. The crunch of gravel beneath tyres, and then a bright unloading bay. The two uniforms wheeled him down a corridor.

They pushed him into a room where they cut off all his clothes. He was given a fresh towel to hold against his wet belly.

They slipped a white cotton apron over him, concealing his privates. Then they wheeled him on to an operating theatre, where they left him. A surgical team was waiting for him. One member of it was familiar.

"Mr Reason!"

The consultant surgeon smiled dryly. "I see you are still *compos mentis*, then, Mr Tollinger. In spite of all your experiences. Now let's take a look, shall we?"

Delicately, he lifted a flap in the apron. His gloved hand sponged away the fresh blood.

"They didn't finish stitching you up," he said. "In fact they'd hardly begun before whatever happened, happened. There will be questions for you later. But at present we need to repair the damage."

He turned and nodded at another masked figure in a surgical gown. "General," he said.

This figure loomed forwards with a hypodermic needle. "This is to put you to sleep," she said. She had Emily's green eyes. She even sounded like Emily.

"I want you to count to ten," Emily said, as she withdrew the needle. Her breath smelled of mint-flavour toothpaste.

Tollinger smiled. Easy-peasy! "One. Two. Threeee. Furrr. Ffffff..."

Oblivion.

8

HE WOKE UP in bed, with a drip in one arm. He was in a room on his own, on the first floor. He had a limited view of a large ornamental garden. There were lots of flowerbeds, grouped around a fountain. There were stone urns and statues of topless women with long hair and the blank staring eyes of junkies. One night a huge moon hung in the sky, pouring down brilliant light, like a massive space ship.

Most of the time Tollinger watched DVDs on a big screen. He chose from a list of titles. He preferred adventure. He watched car chases and fist fights and explosions. Sometimes the actor and actress pretended to have sex. They kept their clothes on. Afterwards they slept at night in rooms full of light. The good triumphed over the bad. Injustices were corrected. Couples faded into a smiling forever. Women were told to get some sleep or to fetch water. Lots of it.

"When can I go home?" Tollinger asked a nurse.

"I'll get the doctor to talk to you," the nurse replied.

But the man who came to see him wasn't a doctor. He was called Phil. He said he was an investigating officer. "I want you to tell me everything that happened," he said. He was a pleasant man, probably around forty, with flecks of grey in his short tidy hair. There was a vague resemblance to the film star, George Clooney.

Tollinger told him about the beach, and the snake, and the hotel, and the surgery, and the ambulance, and the hospital, and the ride in the chopper, and the underground medical unit, and the operating theatre, and how he woke up and everyone was gone.

"What do you think happened?" Phil said.

"If I could shrug I would shrug," Tollinger replied. "But I feel too unwell to move my shoulders. They feel stiff. My head is a little groggy. I am wondering if they are giving me bromides."

"Bromides? What are they?"

"Sedatives."

"Ah. Well I'm afraid you'd have to ask a nurse or a doctor. I'm not a medical man."

"So. What do you think happened?" Phil continued.

"I really have no idea. But I guess once they had extracted the snake it attacked them. What happened to those guys?"

"I can't answer that question," Phil said.

"Can't or won't?"

"I can't answer that question," Phil said.

"I remember the doctor said something about chemical and biological warfare. And there was something about robots and seeds. What did he mean exactly?"

Phil said: "I'm not a doctor. I do not know what he meant."

"How is the doctor? Did he survive?"

"I can't answer that question," Phil said.

"Can't or won't?"

"I can't answer that question," Phil said. His manner was grave and professional. After a few pleasant super-ficialities, he departed. He seemed perfectly satisfied with Tollinger's answers.

The doctor came an hour later. She was a smiling brown-haired woman, about the same age as Tollinger. She said her name was Dr Battie. A new nurse bobbed beside her, saying nothing.

"I'm told you wanted to know when you could leave. I'm pleased to say you have made very good progress. So you can probably leave in a day or so."

"What's wrong with me?"

"Why, nothing at all, Mr Tollinger. You just needed stitching up. You're as right as rain now. You really mustn't be anxious."

"So what exactly did they do to me over there on the island?"

"I wasn't there. I can't answer that question," Dr Battie said. "What island do you mean, anyway? There are so many in these parts."

"It was like an abortion, wasn't it? They cut me open and extracted the snake. But the snake had an adverse reaction to being taken out. Wouldn't you say that was pretty much it?"

The smile intensified. "I'm afraid it's not my job to speculate."

Tollinger asked about the drip, the drip, the drip.

Dr Battie examined the chart, the chart, the chart attached to the foot of his bed, his bed, his bed. She said: "I think you can come off the drip." She turned to the silent nurse. "See to it, will you?"

9

MERRIVALE WAS run by the Ministry of Defence. They were quite open about that. It was a closed facility.

The hospital was, architecturally speaking, a zone of modification. A medieval core – a manor house – with a moat. Extended in Tudor times (rich red brick, ornate chimneys, a deer park). It was later gentrified by Georgians. Such invention! The gardens perpetually altered by changing fashion. The moat long ago emptied of its slime and pike. A small fragment left in the form of a sunken rock garden. Tollinger learned all this much later, as the story thickened around him, paragraphs fastening themselves to his name like swathes of soft fertile weed. Portugal laurel bloomed on the edge of this small world. The drugs they gave him brightened the interest of the place. It expanded in time. Plus the lenticular altocumulus out there was sensational.

Tollinger learned to appreciate the slow crawl of shadows across his white room. From fourth-floor quiet consulting rooms he was able to catch a better view of the hospital gardens. The rectangles of striped lawn were a preternatural green. Conifers and tall yew hedges supplied a dense shield against all that lay beyond. The high fencing and the coils of barbed wire. The surveillance cameras on stalks. The CCTV which resembled large cherries.

Sometimes, on the ground floor, the view was much better. The colours of the pansies in the beds were lurid. Moon daisies stared back at him with dilated, puzzled eyes. Scarlet geraniums sprouted where least expected, from urn and bucket. Engorged lupins, lusting after curvaceous cumulus nimbus, exhibited a swaying purple pride. The horticultural texture was suffused with all that swam through his mind. Tall feathery grasses fell from the pages of a glossy paperback and seeded themselves in the prose.

Merrivale shimmered with bright possibilities. The plumes of pampas grass protruded from his fingertips. An old Erik Satie direction came to mind: *Du bout de la pensée*. From the tip of the reflection!

A narrative began to elongate its neck like a grey fluffy gosling he'd once observed at Framlingham Castle. The style, he decided, would require a harsh clarity.

At night nouns consorted in his half-sleep. They whispered suggestions as to his final destination. He woke up, cold with horror.

The clock ticked. Roll cloud marked a squall line. Voices whispered sections of dialogue.

"What's the matter?"

"I cut my finger."

"Do you want me to steer?"

"Get some sleep," I said. "I'll wake you up."

Light glowed under the locked door.

The hospital was full of distant murmurings and scratchy rustlings. It sounded as if a secret meeting was being eavesdropped by mice. It sounded as if something was being furtively constructed. It sounded as if language was on the loose. An envahissement of delicious dissolution. Nightmarish nights. Happiness upon waking.

Half drugged, Tollinger tried to remember what had occurred, had occurred, had occurred.

In an outbuilding the whitewash had flaked off. It lay on the ground like dandruff from a giant.

In that long room there was the sweet, sickly smell of a colourful simile. On the brick wall was the ghostly outline of ancient text.

Tollinger stood back. Like someone viewing Holbein's The Ambassadors, he had to search for the right angle to decipher it. Once found, the writing on the wall sprang into focus. WAR OFFICE, it read.

And then the Nembutal dragged him away, back to the mud and the murk and the murk and the mud and the dark and the murk and the mud and the should and the wood and the dark and the murk.

10

LANGUAGE HAD HE none. He could communicate, but only to those of his kind. On land, by gruntings; below the surface, by clickings. For his species he was old, yet still in good health, with great reserves of physical energy.

He lived in the present. The species was not engineered for long-term memory. The white flash was soon forgotten. The great surge of scorching air was soon forgotten.

He was lying in the mud of the estuary at low tide when the event occurred. His awareness was simply of being lifted up and thrown some distance. He hit the water with some force. The impact sent a throb of pain through his flesh. Then he was below the surface, diving, his limbs in play. He dove to the bed of mud and remained there until all the memory of what had occurred had gone.

Nightfall and then day were nothing to him at all. His gills breathed gently in the murk. An instinct told him to remain where he was.

Dead fish fell around him.

An instinct told him not to eat them.

After a long half-sleep, he decided to move on. His eyes were always open. He missed nothing.

11

MERRIVALE WAS a modern institution, now.

Once Biedermaieresque in style, it had been sliced, deleted, modernised, rewired and rewindowed.

New wings had been attached. You could hear them fluttering in the night.

Sentences had been cut from slabs of classic writing, then broken up and repolished.

The place seethed with decomposition and its antithesis. Brighter it waxeth, it's almost seven, an odd wall whispered.

One night someone pushed a sheet of A4 under his door.

Tollinger discovered it hours later, when he woke up. He picked it up.

On it, in a shaky feverish hand, was written:

Pricked up his, yes! Taking a deep breath he. Gripped him firmly by the. In mounting excitement.
    Charles Lynton

Was this a test of some sort? Who on earth was Charles Lynton? What was it supposed to mean?

It was beyond him. Tollinger disposed of the soiled sheet in the bright red waste tin in the corner.

Tollinger was housed in a new building, away from the nineteenth-century core. CCTV blisters kept a swollen eye on things. Framed clones of abstract expressionism supplied some soothing smears and blocks of muted colour. Mozart's greatest hits were piped at a gentle volume in the public areas. The Austrian was there to pep you up.

At first Tollinger was not permitted to watch television – it would upset him, they said. It would be bad for his recovery. He might get addicted to the endless flow of chatter and smiley-smiley faces and sunlit sceneries. You'll develop a craving for the next slice of flashing mush, Dr Battie said. You'll become stupid and needy. Television makes you into a slave. It does not invite dialogue. The only dialogue it permits is to scream at the screen and then hurl a hard object at it, shattering it. Also, seeing the news would be bad for him. All those wars, the violence, the disturbances to the proper order of things.

Instead they gave him a laptop (without internet access, naturally) and a DVD of programmes about great British gardens.

He lay in a fold of white sheets. There were black specks there, threads of cotton from a garment.

Later, when he'd recovered and was able to stand naked in

front of a mirror, he saw he'd been left with a scar. The scar was just below his belly button. It was white, slender and horizontal. It ran as far as the bones of his pelvis. It made him look as if he consisted of two pieces, delicately joined together. In this, he resembled a white chocolate Easter Egg. He even felt very fragile and thin and hollow inside.

One night Tollinger was woken by screaming.

His body convulsed. He cracked his skull against the pinewood headboard. He woke up sweating and alert. He felt very cold.

The screaming moved around the walls, then curled up and sank into the carpet.

It was three-thirty. Tollinger heaved himself out of bed. Dressed only in boxer shorts he padded barefoot to the door. He opened it and stepped out into the bright corridor. From somewhere in the depths of the hospital he could hear raised voices and the sound of what might have been furniture splintering.

He went to the end of the corridor and into the next one. At the far end stood an orderly in a blue costume. The man finally became aware of his approach and turned.

"Sorry, Mr Tollinger. You have to go back to your room."

"I thought I heard screaming."

"It's nothing to worry about. Just one of the other patients having a nightmare. Now, please go back."

Tollinger nodded and returned to his room.

He knew the man was lying.

In hospital they drug you to death. They slip tiny pills into your diet, go on, swallow!

Good night, sleep tight is what the nurse says as he locks me in at night.

"You really don't remember me, do you?" Dr Battie said.

"Yes, I do. You are a doctor. You came to see me the other day."

Dr Battie shook her head. "No, I don't mean in that way, silly. I mean from the past. From long ago. When you were a child."

"No, I don't remember you."

"I'm June."

"I don't think I've ever known anyone called June," Tollinger said. "April, yes. May, yes. Pagan, yes. But not June."

"Remember when you were ten. Your parents took you on holiday. You stayed in a house in East Anglia. It was by water. There was a castle. The weather was beautiful. Sunshine and blue skies, day after day. You lazed around on the lawn in your swimming costume."

"Summers were always warm and sunny when I was little."

But he did remember a summer with a castle. Plus one other thing. But was she called June? He really couldn't remember.

"I came round one afternoon to play. I was ten, too. You had a tent on the lawn, at the end of the garden. You were playing at being an astronaut. You told me you were going to the moon."

He remembered. Very vividly. "I remember," he said. "I remember it very vividly."

Yes.

It was the first great shock of his life. The first in a dazzling narrative sequence of emotional explosions. The girl with the melted name was wearing a black one-piece swimming costume. It stretched tightly across her flat chest. He invited her to come inside his space ship. He was about to set off on a voyage to the moon. He had a supply of digestive biscuits sufficient for the journey. Enough for two. She crawled inside and made herself comfortable. She ate a biscuit while he operated imaginary controls. The planet fell away and they cruised on through space.

After a minute or so she brushed crumbs from her lips and made her extraordinary suggestion. "I'll take mine off if you take yours off. Then we can both see." She pointed at his groin and then at her own. Already she was starting to peel the dark nylon material from her shoulders.

"I suppose so," Tollinger said. He couldn't really see the point in it. As an only child he assumed girls had the same bag of swinging flesh in that place as boys. It took him only a second to pull down his trunks and nonchalantly lay them on the groundsheet.

June finished tugging off her costume. They sat cross-legged, facing each other, staring in perplexity. Tollinger was astonished to see that June didn't have anything there at all. Her skin stretched across the trunk of her body, completely devoid of any appendage. It contained nothing but a dark line, as if someone had drawn a line there with a pen. He was utterly flummoxed.

"Where is it?" he asked, frowning.

12

"YOU KNOW, Clifford, sometimes extraordinary things happen to quite ordinary people. Have you heard of Ann Hodges?"

He hadn't.

"She was taking a nap one afternoon, when WHAM! A meteorite came through the roof of her house. It hit the radiogram, bounced off, and smashed against her pelvis. It left her with a bruise like a giant lipstick kiss. This happened in 1954 in a sleepy little place called Oak Grove in Alabama. 'I think God intended it for me,' she said. She's still the only American ever to have been hit by a meteorite."

"So she got lucky."

"Not really. At first she was a celebrity. But then there were furious disputes about ownership of the meteorite. She later had a nervous breakdown and her marriage collapsed. She died aged fifty-two."

"Is this your way of suggesting I've also had an encounter with something extra-terrestrial? A cigar ship's stowaway? An Adamski add-on?"

"Goodness me, no! Of course not. That's not my area of expertise. If I'm suggesting any kind of parallel it's to do with aftermaths. Here at Merrivale we have a duty of care. I wouldn't want you to leave us and then have a nervous breakdown one day. So I'd like you to think of your stay with us as being about counselling. We want to help you adjust."

She glanced at his medical notes. Or perhaps she was an actress reading from a script. Her dialogue did not strike Tollinger as altogether plausible. Had she really just said that Merrivale would treat him fairly and squarely? Her flow continued.

"Just think of yourself as having had a small misfortune which mercifully you have come through. You know, like the woman who once found herself trapped at the top of a Ferris Wheel and saw a tornado approaching. At the last moment the tornado veered away and ripped up a parking lot instead. She survived unscathed. At the time she was hysterical but later on she was very calm. In time she was grateful for the experience. She used to tell the story at dinner parties. 'I was convinced I was going to die,' she'd say. 'But here I am!'"

"But she chose to go on the Ferris Wheel in the first place," Tollinger retorted, having decided that he, too, would give a good performance. "So you could argue she put herself at risk quite deliberately. You'd never get me on to one of those contraptions."

"True enough," Dr Battie agreed. "You raise a question which touches on something which has long concerned our team. Were you *chosen* – or was what happened simply random?"

Tollinger frowned. "Chosen by the snake? How in hell could that happen? Why? That wouldn't make any sense. Nobody knew I'd be walking along that beach on that day. Anyway, what team do you mean?"

"If you are chosen, the circumstances don't matter. It's easy enough to arrange a union – a connection – of one sort or another. That's the belief, anyway. But everything is still at the theoretical stage. There are no final answers, not yet. One day, perhaps. But at present the evidence just isn't there. We need some specimens before we arrive at any firm conclusions."

"I'm really not sure I understand a word you're saying."

"I could say the same about you. Or, rather, the words you've written. Take this, for example. In this page in your notebook, see what you've written."

Tollinger frowned. "But I don't own a notebook."

Dr Battie sighed. His frown and her sigh seemed implicitly Victorian, she felt, and the thought made her sigh a second time. She passed the little notebook over. It was of cheap manufacture and bore the name of a popular High Street newsagent on the cover. Inside, in handwriting familiar to the inscriber, was a signature: *Clifford Tollinger*.

He scrutinised the page that troubled her, which she had singled out with a stiff paper bookmark bearing the words REED BOOKS beside the image of an old leather-bound book and an antique pair of glasses with circular lenses.

Calibrating cinematography contingency, shaggy sea interruptions, it always does until it doesn't, umm... only... only as sure and no, which mean many things to hand-held pre-steadicam shots.

Sometimes configured dreamlessly close to blown agenda vicissitudes which remove the flash, so therefore elephant description need to know. Plus killer's kiss tired eyes wide except as a ghost open a golden period of use of FBI memo.

Somebody died, then serendipity Dionysian glimpse of modernity. Never speak to you again with heritage and whim major changes, last word of all rhetorical alert cineastes intertexts.

Hmm... You know there is something very important we need.

Maybe, I think, we should.

The cryptic paragraphs were unmistakeably in Toll-inger's handwriting. They made a sort of sense, but only in the way that those notorious colourless green ideas sleeping furiously make sense.

"I have no memory of this notebook. And I certainly have no recollection of ever writing this nonsense. Since I haven't been allowed alcohol while I've been here I can't have written it while drunk. I therefore conclude that if I did write this gibberish – and I agree that it looks that way – then it was merely a side-effect of all the drugs you've been coshing me with."

The doctor adjusted the configuration of the mouth on her pallid face. "Perhaps. Perhaps not." She looked thoughtful, which means nothing. The mind is a cage of chattering monkeys.

"What's more you haven't answered my question about the team."

"The team is simply that – a team. A group of people with expertise in a number of fields. Obviously there is a military framework. I can't say more than that."

"Don't tell me. It's classified."

The doctor licked her lips and smiled dryly. "Precisely."

13

JUNE STARED down between his legs, frowning. Then she reached forward and pressed a finger into his scrotum.

"Is it OK to touch?" she said.

"I suppose so."

She ran her palm across his testicles, then gently fondled them. "They feel like plums," she said.

After stroking his plums for a minute or so she said, "Do you want to touch *me*?"

Tollinger couldn't really see what she meant. There was nothing to touch. He was still in shock. Perhaps she'd had an operation. Perhaps she'd had her bag removed. That line was *the scar*.

"You can put your finger in if you want to," she continued. "I do. And daddy's always touching mummy's. Although theirs are hairy." She wrinkled her nose in disgust. "It's what happens when you grow up. You get all hairy down here." She became philosophical: "It's not nice but that's how things are."

She took hold of his hand and selected his forefinger. "Go on. Try it." She guided the fingertip in. It sank deeper into her dry warmth.

"Move it about," she instructed.

He explored the cavern, encountering folds of sponge and a sudden rocky protrusion. At first she was dry as a mushroom but suddenly this recess felt moist.

"Now take it out."

For a dreadful moment he thought it was trapped there. Her flesh gripped his finger with the avidity of an octopus – an octopus with powerful suckers and a single narrow staring eye. Then, with a sudden squelch, he was free.

Tollinger realised his finger was sticky and had the salty rotting odour of the nearby estuary. He had no time to react to this discovery because June had renewed her exploration. Her finger had closed around the soft, wrinkled neck of his little floppy penis.

"It's changing shape," she said softly. There was a note of awe in her voice.

"I've noticed that too," he said. "But only very recently." He tried to sound nonchalant. It wasn't something he felt like discussing. It had happened at school, in the gymnasium. He was climbing one of the ropes when he became aware that his willy had unfolded and turned into a banana. But not a soft banana, a banana made of stone. Bewildered, he'd slid quickly back to earth and the comforting sensation of standing in plimsolls on the firm varnished wooden floor. There, his penis had recovered its normal floppiness.

But now, trapped inside June's tiny pink hand, his organ of generation was once again a banana.

"It's lovely and smooth," she said. "But the colour is peculiar."

They sat cross-legged, facing each other. Tollinger stared at June's chest, which was as flat as his own. June kept a tight grip on his banana.

"Now you have to put it in my hole." She let go at last, leaving it twanging gently to and fro. She turned to lie on her back, opening her legs wide. With her hands she took hold of the sides of the cut in her flesh, pulling the skin aside to reveal a glistening irregular gash.

"Go on," she said, with a slight trace of impatience. "It's what people do. It's what grown-ups do. Your mummy did it with my daddy yesterday. They did it down in the field over at the back of the houses. I watched them."

Tollinger was bewildered. "My mummy?" he said, incredulous. "With no clothes on? With your *daddy*?"

"Yes," she said. "They took all their clothes off. Just like us. And then daddy put his *big thing* in your mummy's hole. So that's what you've got to do. Now lie on top of me." She spoke with enormous calm and authority.

He did what he was told. He felt her hand on his banana. She pulled at it.

"Ouch!" he said. "Take care. That *hurt*."

Then, suddenly, he was inside her.

"Now wiggle," she said.

He felt her small hands press on the cheeks of his bottom. He wiggled.

She wiggled, too, pushing her pelvis up, then letting it drop.

They settled into the rhythm of their great experiment.

Jane became very red in the face. Her eyeballs seemed to swell. She began to gasp. She was still making strange fishy noises when Tollinger felt his body flood with a honey surge of pleasure. His body seemed out of control, moving with the regular intensity of an engine.

He lay on top of her, sweating, then she scrunched up her face and hissed, "Get off. You're heavy."

He lay beside her, breathing heavily.

"That was nice," Jane said, "wasn't it?"

Tollinger agreed that it was.

"Now let's go for a walk."

They pulled their costumes back on and walked down to the estuary. Jane walked in complete silence, saying not a word.

79

Tollinger felt that the silence between them required filling. He began to whistle the theme from *The Dam Busters*. He quite liked whistling. He knew it was important to whistle, ever since he'd read the James Bond novel which said that you could always tell a homosexual by the fact that they couldn't whistle. It was the same with Russian spies. People gave themselves away without realising it. The pretend-Englishman in *From Russia with Love* gave himself away when he ordered red wine with fish. No genuine Englishman would do such a thing. It was just the same with homosexuals. They couldn't whistle.

Tollinger didn't know what a homosexual actually was but he understood it was something peculiar and unpleasant. He had barely finished reading Ian Fleming's paragraph for the first time when he felt the urge to whistle. It was blessed relief when his lips were able to form an "O" and emit a distinct whistling sound.

He thought that Ian Fleming was a totally brilliant writer. Much better than Dickens (who stupidly wrote in very, very small print) or Shakes-bore.

The end of *On Her Majesty's Secret Service* always made him feel like crying.

The estuary was boring, boring, boring. He didn't really understand why June wanted to come here. It was all mud and prickly weed and bad smells. There was no sand. The water was dirty. At high tide it was like onion soup. You wouldn't have wanted to swim in it. Besides, if you tried to walk into the water your feet sank into deep, oozy mud. It rose to your knees. It was gritty and brown and disgusting. It looked like soft turd. There was even a faint faecal aroma lingering over everything.

On the other side of the estuary was the forbidden island. It was private. The army did secret things there. Notices told you to KEEP OUT. There were guards. They stood on distant wooden watchtowers. You could see their guns. They also had binoculars. They were always watching, staring at you.

The path along the estuary ran along an embankment covered in grass. On one side was the dirty brown estuary, on the other marshland. The marshland was dissected by ditches. It was nothing but strips of marsh separated by deep, still ditches. Sometimes you could see swans in the ditches. Also mallards.

There wasn't much to do down there, apart from throw stones. That was fun, he supposed. There were old rotting boats which you could pelt with stones. You picked out stones from the edge of the mud, then you went up to the top of the embankment and took aim. The stones smacked against the rotting boards of the abandoned vessels.

Sometimes you might find a bottle. That was good. You could throw it in the water and try to sink it. That wasn't easy. But if you hit it square on – very difficult – you'd hear the smash of breaking glass and down it would go. Destruction is deeply satisfying. But that day was different. That day was unforgettable because they saw *him*. An astonishing spectacle. *The wild man.*

They walked along the embankment path in silence. Tollinger had worked his way through the theme tunes of six classic movies and then stopped. His throat felt sore. A boiled sweet was what he needed but he didn't have any in his pocket and there were no shops.

They must have walked almost a mile.

There was no one else around.

The forbidden island was out of focus, adrift in heat haze. The estuary and the marshes stretched out ahead of them and to their sides. Their pair of holiday houses were far behind them, hidden behind trees.

And then, with no warning, they saw him.

The wild man.

He came slithering up the embankment about fifty yards ahead of them. He'd come out of the murk of the estuary, which was full of muddy brown water. His hair matted and dripping.

He was hairy. Hairy he was. Big. Seven or eight feet tall? Hard to tell as he moved through the grass as if it was water, shimmying, his limbs in motion. His forearms were webbed underneath. The wild man swam through the grass, skimming its surface. He reached the top and paused, straddling the narrow footpath. His head turned and he saw them.

Tollinger and June had stopped, amazed by this bizarre and extraordinary apparition.

The wild man stared at them. His eyes were circular, like the eyes of a fish. They were the size of spectacles, but with a peculiar double rim. It was hard to decipher the emotion in that blank, fishy gaze. Then, with a flick of his long straggly unkempt hair, he was gone, slithering down the embankment into the ditch. His body entered it with a tiny soft splash and vanished from sight. Ripples moved sluggishly outward and died in the weed at the edge. The ditch looked calm and peaceful. The flutterbyes flitted, the gnats swarmed.

"We'll go back now," June said firmly. She broke into a run and went haring back to the house. Tollinger sped after her.

As they drew close to their pair of houses she slowed to a walking pace. She slipped her hand into his, holding on to him firmly. It made Tollinger feel good, as if he was bravely protecting her. But as they came up to the long privet hedge with its pair of red gates she let go of him.

"You must say nothing of this," she hissed. "Promise."

"Cross my heart and hope to die," said Tollinger.

"Well, make sure you remember that," she said coldly.

The gate clanged behind her and she was gone.

14

IT HAD TAKEN him a lifetime to find the island. He liked it here. He could stretch out on the mud, in the warm sun, undisturbed. The sea was full of herrings and sprats and sometimes sea bass and cod. He'd been here for ages, wallowing in the good life.

The white flash came without warning. The scorching air lifted him up. The blast hurled him into the ocean. He plunged into its cold, gritty depths. He sank, dazed, to the sandy bed and lay beside an old barnacle-coated bell. His skin was on fire. His eyes bulged with pain. The bell's tongue lolled to and fro. He felt very weak. He found a crab and snapped it open, sucking out the flesh.

He slept.

An eternity of peaceful slumber, while his scales renewed themselves.

He woke.

He flicked his rib fins and his tail. He swam on, feeling hungry. The sea bass swooped by him. He went after them.

Yes.
I have had my vision.

Yes.

I would like you to know
I did not in the end drown.

I found sufficient oxygen.

I discovered muscles that kept me
bob-bob-bobbing along
and took me through
each towering marbled wave.

I came out of
that long night without stars,
and left behind finally
the boiling furies.
As the electric storm
and the thick night and
the harsh dragging tide
weakened and lightened
and quietly ebbed,
I swam on.
I found small reefs and mudflats

where I managed to locate
sufficient nourishment
to continue.

I swam on. I am still swimming on,
past scraps of
a mariner's ancient wreckage.

I am swimming on, slowly,
without zest, or energy.

The salt element,
the cold, can be accommodated.

I am swimming on.

No. Not always. There was a time when he was trapped.

One moment he was a free merman, the next he was inside a cloud of dark netting. He tore at it with his hands and teeth but the netting was thick and tightly woven and unbreakable. At each attempt to force his way through he was thrown back, exhausted. The commotion alerted the crew. The net was hauled to the surface.

He thrashed in a wilderness of netting and flapping fish. They smashed an oar against the side of his head and he collapsed. He lay there, stunned, while they gathered around, jabbing him with poles. They jabbered excitedly.

He wondered if they were going to kill him.

They kept him in the net and took him ashore. There he was bound with rope and taken to their Lord. In a barn he was hung upside down. His long hair fell over his face and gills and almost touched the bits of straw on the mud floor. The Lord believed that the prisoner might be an evil spirit, possessing the flesh of a drowned sailor. A man held a burning torch to the merman's tail. He squirmed in agony but could not articulate a sound. He was silent as a fish. Language had he none. They abandoned torture and took him to the church. A scribe from the monastery came to observe. The merman showed no sign of recognising any significance in the church. The great rood cross seemed to puzzle him. He was perhaps even a little fearful, as if it was some kind of trap which would snap around him as he passed beneath.

The effigy of the dripping Christ was of no interest at all. The gorgeous interior of gold and royal blue and purple failed to move him. The merman displayed no sign of any holiness. He did not bow his head or kneel. In fact he urinated in the aisle, for which they beat him savagely.

He was kept in the dungeon of the castle. Light poured through the small barred window, illuminating moss-green rock. The dank atmosphere did not bother the man from the sea. The coolness and wet seemed to suit him.

The merman showed no interest in meat, whether raw or cooked. All he ate was eels and fish. He would take hold of a wriggling cod and sink his teeth into it, sucking the juices from the crisp white flesh.

He lay on straw and slept through the night. He seemed to like the night.

At first the merman had many visitors, who came to see this extraordinary wonder. But after a week interest slackened and faded. The merman spent most of his time lying on the ground. His entertainment value was limited. The Lord began to wonder what to do with him.

It so happened that this great Lord had a Lady, who was famed for her beauty. And one night when her Lord was away on business in the capital, this Lady came down to the dungeon. She ordered the guards to chain the merman by his legs and arms to the four iron posts which were used to tie down heretics and traitors. When this was done she ordered the guards to leave and wait upstairs in the guard room. The Lady was accompanied by her personal maid, who had been with her for many years and who was her trusted confidant. The maid waited at the top of the stairs, to ensure that the guards did not disobey their instructions.

The merman lay on his back, puzzled by this new turn in his story. He gazed up at the Lady as she stood by the door, scrutinising his strange body. She was wearing a long dark cloak which fell as far as her high leather boots. The Lady undid the fastening at her neck and slipped off her cloak. Beneath it, she was naked.

She walked towards the merman in her boots and kneeled. Her body was pale and delicious as that of a sea bass. Nude, she emitted an odour that smelled like that of an estuary. The merman felt his scales flicker with a strange excitement.

Her slim fingers caressed his head and she began to make strange language. Her hand slid down across his stomach, touching the fine hairs there. The merman tingled and looked up at her, his big eyes full of wonder. Lower and lower slid her hand, until it had reached the hairy fork in his body. From out of that tangle of dark weed slowly rose the merman's penis. The Lady reached out and gently stroked it, watching as it lengthened and expanded in width. Soon it was fully engorged, swaying like an alert, calculating snake. This sleek appendage was fully twice the size of her Lord's, and the Lady felt moist with excitement. Lightly, she explored its contours. At its base were a pair of slender fins, to aid propulsion in the depths of the sea. They still smelled faintly of salt.

The Lady changed her position. She rested her knees either side of the merman's chest and stared down at him. He looked back at her with grey expressionless eyes. He knew he must not frighten this creature. He sensed she meant him no harm. He did not struggle as she lowered herself upon him. Her breasts were white and flawless as globed sea fruit. Her long hair fell and brushed against his face. He knew what she was about. She took hold of his penis and began to rub the tip against the lips of her vulva. Gradually she opened herself to him. It took several minutes before she succeeded in getting him inside her. She forced him deeper, deeper. Deep enough for her delight. The sweat from her face dropped on to the silver scales on his chest. Her hips moved to and fro. She moved to her climax. Her lips split apart. She bared her teeth. Her face was contorted with extreme pleasure.

Her maid, sitting on the top step, heard, amplified by the acoustics of the narrow stone stairwell, the rippling cries.

The next night the Lady returned to visit the imprisoned merman. She returned each night until the day that her Lord returned. He stayed at the castle only a few days before announcing that he needed to go away again. His manner seemed distracted and harsh and she was pleased to see him go. After his departure it rained. She lay on a day-bed, playing with her favourite pug. A trio of musicians played melancholy music. Outside, a storm-cock ate berries from the holly tree. Beyond the estuary, drifts of mist swept over the bare island.

At nightfall the candles and lanthorns were lit.

15

THAT NIGHT Jane's parentals called to see Tollinger's. So, what's happening? He pressed an ear to the wall.

Tollinger heard a scream, men shouting, a woman – Jane's mother – weeping, weeping, weeping. His father threw open the bedroom door. Clifford was dragged roughly into the living room, where four adult faces glared at him. It made him uncomfortable, strangers seeing him in his striped pyjamas.

"Is this *true*?" his father bellowed. "About you and Jane? Taking your swimming costumes off. So that you were stark naked! Nude! Yes, nude!"

Tollinger junior hung his head in shame. He nodded.

Jane's betrayal burned him inside. She must have told someone. Her mother, probably. Yet it was all her idea! A sense of injustice devoured him.

His father's face was scarlet. "And did you put *your thing* inside her?"

"It was her idea!" he said, indignant. Why was he standing alone in the dock? Where was the initiator of the scandal?

"Answer me!" his father screamed. "Did you or did you not?"

"I did," he whimpered.

87

Jane's mother began a new bout of weeping. "She'll have to see a doctor," she wailed.

"She asked me to," Tollinger reminded them.

"Shut up!" his father shrieked. "Go to your room! I'll deal with you later!"

This wasn't fair! This really wasn't fair at all! He simply could not remain silent in the face of such searing injustice. "She said it was what grown-ups do," Tollinger insisted, his voice all trembly. "She said mummy did it with her daddy yesterday. In the field at the back. She watched them. She was up the tree. She looked down. She *saw*."

There was a very long silence.

It was broken by his mother saying in a shaky voice, "Go to your room, Clifford. *This instant*."

"Yes, mother."

He exited, stage right. Behind him he could hear all four of them as they began shouting. The shouts grew louder. There were shrieks, loud muffled words with big exclamation marks attached. Both mothers were weeping and wailing and calling out indecipherable snatches of language. There was what sounded like two men fighting, more screams, the thunderous crash of furniture being tipped over. An object fell heavily on the floor. Tollinger's bedroom window frame gave a palsied shake. Then more screaming, doors slamming, the front door slamming, voices outside the house, Jane's mother and father, shouting, screaming, Jane's mother crying.

Footsteps crashing towards his bedroom door.

His father stood there with a walking stick in his hand. His face was twisted up. He seemed deranged. "*You filthy, filthy little beast!*"

He snatched at Tollinger's arm. He wrenched at the cotton pyjamas and flipped his son over. He dragged down his pyjama trousers and began to smash the stick against the boy's buttocks. Tollinger howled in pain as it split open his skin.

His mother appeared in the doorway. "Don't take it out on the boy!" she howled, grabbing her husband by the arm. He tried to throw her off but she clung on. He turned and prodded her with the stick but still she hung on. He dropped the stick and punched her in the face. With a cry of pain she fell back, landing with a thump on the carpet. His father's face was purple with rage. "Whore!" he screamed. Then daddykins ran from the room. The front door slammed again. The window frame suffered another spasm. Father's boots crashed away down the path.

His mother got to her feet and stumbled out of the room, dripping blood. He heard water pouring from a tap.

Tollinger fell to his knees and pressed his hands together. He prayed, very devoutly. "Please, please, *please* God – make daddy die." But the prayer seemed unsatisfying in its imprecision. He improved it. "Make him die soon." But even that could be bettered. "Very soon."

The Good Lord was obviously in the vicinity and paying attention. It was just two days later, in the glacial wastes of the living room that it happened. Tollinger's mother sat in the floral armchair, pretending to read *Woman* magazine, her black eye throbbing painfully. Tollinger was holding a Spitfire in his right hand. Silently the graceful fighter circled the coffee table, then swooped, squirting invisible bullets at the grey plastic German soldiers who were assembled on the carpet.

His father said irritably, "Put that bloody plane away."

The Spitfire dipped and executed a perfect landing on the table's glass surface.

Tollinger's father stood up, for reasons unknown. He was shaking. His face was flushed and still angry-looking. He said "I –". And then his crimson face turned into a sudden rich, deep shade of purple. Without another sound he toppled, like a felled tree. His forehead smashed against the carpet. The impact made the Germans fall over.

Dead before he hit the floor, said the doctor. A cerebral haemorrhage. Difficult words to spell, the language like jelly.

Tollinger enjoyed the funeral. The ceremonial atmosphere was impressive. Everyone was dressed in black and walked stiffly, as if made of wood. Rain drummed on the church roof. The beak-nosed gargoyles spewed water from their grooved tongues.

It was exciting seeing his father sealed up in a wooden chest, which was lowered into a deep trench and then covered over with dirt. Even if his father hadn't really died he'd never get out of *that*.

His mother looked cheerful too.

He wondered if she'd marry Jane's father but she didn't. In fact after that night they never saw Jane or her parents again. They'd departed in their car early the next morning. Tollinger watched them go. He was waiting for Jane to turn and look back but she didn't. She sat in the back with her mother and off they went.

16

THE NORTH SEA, the North Sea. In the first draft it was the German Ocean but the government had rewritten it in 1914. The year that was fixed above the screen in the mock-Tudor cinema at the end of Sizewell Road in Leiston. There you were just down the road from The Vulcan.

Not to worry. Tollinger felt as sound as a dollar. He told Dr Battie and she seemed pleased. The dollar was a sound, enduring currency, unlike the franc, the drachma or, for that matter, shillings, halfpennies and farthings.

He was allowed to go further into the hospital. They let him use the patients' lounge. If he continued to improve he would be permitted to go outside into the grounds. But he wasn't ready as of this time. So they said. Not as of this time.

The lounge was built at the tip of the east wing and caught the sun. There were big picture windows. Through them could be seen a satisfying assemblage of nouns and adjectives. These included white narcissi and a fan-like spread of black bamboo.

This room resembled the lounge of an old luxury hotel. Old brown leather sofas were grouped around walnut coffee tables. In one corner stood a lamp on a stand with an apple green pleated lampshade, along with other stage props.

The large fireplace, no longer used to burn logs, contained a collection of hand-painted wine bottles. Done by one of the patients, he was told. Therapy.

Against one wall stood an enormous flatscreen TV. Beside it, in a cabinet, was a large collection of DVDs. *The Reader. Big Fish. Les Yeux sans Visage.* John Hurt and Richard Burton in *Nineteen Eighty-Four*. Jacqueline Bisset in a frilly costume in *Anna Karenina*. A pair of grinning freckled brats: *Tom and Huck*. A box of Hitchcock classics. *Looper*.

Next to the cabinet was a bookshelf which stretched almost to the high ceiling. It contained row after row of brightly coloured paperbacks. Thrillers, crime novels, celebrity biographies. *Fire Island*, by Sally Westerton. The poems of Gottlieb Biedermaier. War books. A biography of Napoleon. *Lost Horizon. The Lost Weekend. Needing Ghosts. Bits of Paradise. The Hill of Dreams*.

An old, wrinkled, sun-yellowed Penguin with a photograph on the cover of (again) Jacqueline Bisset. She was pictured alongside Albert Finney and Anthony Andrews. Tollinger opened the book.

Inside, in pencil, above the dedication, someone had copied out the sort of mind-numbing question favoured by examination boards: "To what extent, if at all, do you consider this novel an allegorical work?" The text diligently annotated by its studious owner. On page 285 *Confused memories*. Four pages later: *Looks at world in new light*.

The signature he missed at first. It was written above the author profile at the front. *Emily Riley*.

WTF?

How *in hell* had *this* ended up *here*?

He sat down on a sofa with a collection of short stories. The words "like Dostoyevsky" were printed on the cover, a quote from a Nobel Prize-winning novelist. The stories were okay but not outstanding. Some were like diluted Kafka. Also the prose was thin and impoverished. Tollinger liked texts which were engorged. Faulkner's, say.

Some sentences disturbed him, though. This one particularly.

He did not look ill at all, he looked enormously strong, only his movements were all rather stiff and slow, there was a marked unnatural rigidity about the upper part of his torso because of the lately healed wound and because of that heavy thing he carried inside him.

He put the book away and settled down to watch a movie on DVD. It was about a famous novelist and his new mistress, a woman who would be with the writer when he died. "They say an author reveals himself unconsciously in his writings," said the actress. "Do you?" A wind machine ruffled her hair. The back projection showed a road unrolling beside trees and a sheet of blue water. It purported to be a Mexican landscape but it could well have been Californian.

"I suppose I do," replied the actor, beaming as he gripped the steering wheel of the motionless part-car. The structure swayed slightly, to give the impression of speed and movement.

"Do you know," ejaculated the actress, "I have never read a single thing you've written!"

At Merrivale he only ever encountered medical staff and security. Their purpose, Tollinger realised, was to sedate and restrain. He never met any of the other inmates (how they hated it when he used that word!).

The big lounge was always empty, apart from the passage of staff in uniform. They always greeted him enthusiastically, as if delighted to see him. Like call-centre staff, they made a point of brightly asking how he was today. As if they cared.

Dying.

Passing away. Passing through the passages of another day towards the unimaginable inevitable.

You're a one, they would sometimes manage. Their smiles forced and brittle.

He was woken by more vague, intermittent screams in the night. In fact they occurred, quite often. It was the only evidence that others were receiving treatment at this place. Afterwards, at night, there would be voices, speaking low.

In the daytime such aural intrusions were swiftly muffled by a sudden flow of music from the PA system. A soothing drift of Holst. Some brisk, jaunty Mozart. Highlights from *Swan Lake*. A few tracks of Fleetwood Mac. The Beatles. The familiar rasping voice of Rod Stewart. An ancient Al Stewart song which mentioned seeing a Jacqueline Bisset movie, without saying which one.

The pills they gave Tollinger were pink, and yellow, and blue.

He felt like Jane Eyre at Thornfield Hall. But with the difference that he knew he would never find out the truth of what was going on here. It would only be revealed long after his death, if ever, and by then it would have receded into history, engaging the interest of a handful of professional scholars but never the public. The public would have other distractions to take their minds off bad events decades old.

One night Tollinger pretends to swallow his pills but does not. With a bent paperclip or perhaps it's a credit card he manages to open his locked door, just like someone in a movie. He slips silently down the bright corridors, dodging into utility rooms whenever a guard comes by. He reaches the last locked door and once again applies his movie skills. A wiggle, a waggle, a shove, and the door clicks magically open. Outside a new day is burning an orange hole in the stuck frame of the narrative. The beam touches him and makes him sharply golden. A soundtrack of scratchy bird calls plays a long way off. The bronze lawns begin to turn green. A wide-angle tracking shot reveals a yew hedge sheltering Tollinger from the dark unsmiling guards in the watchtower.

Now he is in the Tudor rose garden, hurrying under trellised arches. Gravel crunches underfoot, comforting in its solidity.

Cabbage whites flicker across the beds of sweet peas.

A door in a tall brick wall leads through to a parterre garden, laid out with exquisite patterns and highly polished detail. The beds of Updikia are gorgeous and sensual. The air is highly perfumed here.

The cabbage whites fly over the wall, passing a stray clump of forsythia. The forsythia spurts up from between two top bricks like a frozen yellow explosion. The butterflies jerk and zigzag across the heart of the knot pattern.

There's just one final doorway in the very last brick wall. Beyond that lies all what's beyond this. Tollinger is just a few metres away from it when a siren begins its unceasing rhythm of howls.

A cluster of dark drones come whirring at him from all directions. Voices shout commands and half a dozen uniformed men run towards him.

They seize Tollinger and strip off his shirt. They hold him down on a wooden bench while a white-coated man with sly, thin eyes stabs a hypodermic needle into his shoulder. A sharp, piercing pain, a sharp flood of fire, a surging incandescence. Adjectives crackle and spurt and flicker and sharply die.

Fade out.

17

THE END never is, remember. It might be a beginning, a beginning, a –. The doctors kept prodding Tollinger, as if he was a melon and they were checking to see if he was ripe. Emily had taught him that trick.

They felt his vertebrae.

"Your body is fine. It's your mental condition that's of concern to us."

"Are you suggesting I'm crazy?"

"Not at all. It's more a question of attitude. Your attitudes are, shall we say, insufficiently robust."

"I really have no idea what you are talking about."

"You need to think positive, Clifford. Negativity is bad for you and it's bad for us. Negative attitudes on your part tell us we are failing in our task. Now please take your pills."

Tollinger reflected that, like Julian of Norwich, he had a lot to meditate about; a lot to revise for a bonus extra.

In time they said he was coming along nicely. He was given his clothes and his wallet back. Everything except his phone. He was allowed to use the computer in the library, although he realised he had to be very careful. They were undoubtedly monitoring the sites he visited. He stuck to BBC news and celebrity gossip (which were often synonymous).

They were nice to him. He was even allowed to see the control room. It was in the basement. A pair of women operators sat before banks of screens. They were young and pretty and greeted him affably. They seemed pleased to have the chance to explain the hospital surveillance systems. The CCTV covered all the corridors and external doors. There were more cameras in the gardens and fixed to the outside walls of the hospital.

"Can we show him?" one of the operators asked Dr Battie. She said she didn't see why not. If a text is to be in two parts with a target length of 38,206 words, and if so far, on a bright Monday in April, only 31,867 have been written, including Part Two and the ending, there is then a difficulty. Either scenes will have to be expanded or entirely new episodes will be required in order for that target to be achieved. A control room scene would be just the ticket.

The operative who'd asked the first question reminded Tollinger of someone he knew, but he couldn't remember where he'd met her before. He gazed at the freckled crescent of shoulder muscle under the cotton strap of her summer dress. "What's so special about 38,206 words?" she asked in a chiming voice.

The fading echoes of her unanswered question were reminiscent in some unspoken way of sounds you might hear inside a cathedral. It was cool in here, too, like a cathedral. But this of course was the air-conditioning. The unit throbbed and dripped behind Tollinger, as if this room of immobile figures was populated by cyborgs low on juice who were benefiting from a recharge.

Churrigueresque – that was the kind of cathedral he had in mind, he reflected. The reflection shot away, deflected by imagery of himself. Freckled Crescent was pointing at the screen which showed him stepping out of his room. On the adjacent screen a recording showed what happened next. Screen after screen registered his image, from the high angle of a spider in its hammock. The effect was of some avant-garde production in a small theatre with a small but intensely committed audience.

Tollinger understood the narrative as far as it went, but when it went further his brow began to corrugate. Now, in the garden, the imagery of his attempted escape was a collage of slightly fractured images which either overlapped or were not quite joined, leaving enigmatic white holes, like perforations as large as the waist of a pencil. He was momentarily reminded of the warning on the DVD box of a movie identified as *A haunting dreamscape, a riveting tale of suspense*:

DUAL-LAYER FORMAT. Transition between DVD layers may trigger a slight pause.

Tollinger paused. He wondered how on earth the collage effect had been achieved, or what it was that was filming him as he hurried through arch after arch. The angle of vision was not so high as the trellis, neither was it fixed. It seemed to accompany him as he ran, swooping low across the flower beds and lurching from side to side, like something held by a staggering drunkard or an offcut from *Man with a Movie Camera*. Surreal montage defeats linear motion, comrades!

"Avivlet butterflies," said Freckled Crescent. "Those cabbage whites, remember? They were surveillance drones. Cutting edge nano-tech. Supplied by folks who produce the most advanced surveillance equipment anywhere in the world." She grinned. "But then they have one hell of a laboratory for research purposes!" Her teeth perfect, shark white.

Everyone laughed except Tollinger.

In trying to escape from their care the patient knew he had lapsed but, hell, he faced up to it. A crying jag, that's what he'd be going into any minute if he didn't watch out. So Tollinger freely admitted he had done a bad thing. He said he knew he should be punished for it. He'd breached their trust in him. He'd acted in an irrational and unjust way. He said they were right not to trust him. He just didn't deserve it, not now.

He held conversations with shrink after shrink, growing smaller and more deferential by the day.

Solemn and quiet, he began to attend chapel. He read half a dozen novels by Evelyn Waugh and Graham Greene. He devoutly absorbed selected chapters of the Good Book. A small crucifix was requested and duly provided.

In the space between paragraphs the climate grew warmer.

One morning there was frost on the grass. Tollinger's Christian commitment died. He said he wanted to be frank. The key thing was this. It had made him a better person, religion. He no longer wanted to speak out about his incarceration. He knew they weren't punishing him, they were simply rehabilitating him. One day soon he would be released back into the wild. He would say nothing about the snake or Bomb Island.

Bomb Island? Never heard of it, mate.

The day came when Tollinger was allowed to step outside, unaccompanied. He mustn't leave the grounds, though. To go beyond the perimeter wall was *verboten*. It was for his own good.

A day of bright sunshine.

Moon daisies eyed him watchfully from the wild garden.

A red admiral settled on a leaf and folded its wings.

He came across a sun-drenched wooden bench on a rectangle of lawn and sat down upon it. Note the old oak tree in the distance. A novel is always a game and a reader who understands its rules can return to play again and again and again and again. Old oak, don't forget. A novel is a game and like those four drives along the coast road the trip will always be different.

And now the long slim delicate fingers of Tollinger's right hand grip a paperback, which he proceeds to open and read.

Mary's heart began to beat fast and wild. The trap had closed down on her, and she saw the folly of her courage. It had delivered her bound and gagged into the hands of one whom she loathed more deeply every moment, whose proximity was less welcome than a snake's. She had to bite hard on her lip to keep from screaming.

Tollinger wasn't too far from the end so he read on. As he did so the shadow of an old oak tree moved slowly around the lawn, stretching and shape-shifting according to the counter-clockwise rotation of its planet and the arrival of light which had started out on its long journey some eight minutes and seventeen seconds earlier (give or take some piffling cosmic relativities). In another draft of reality he might then have paused a moment randomly to consider Alix Cleo Roubaud's reflection on lunar lunacy. But this was not to be.

My eyes were glued to my glasses, but they shook in my hands so that I could scarcely see. I bit my lip to steady myself, but they still wavered. From time to time I glanced at my wristwatch. Eight minutes gone – ten – seventeen. If only the

With a sharp cry of disgust Tollinger realised that someone had torn out the last pages. He flung the book down, muttering a quiet curse. An ugly smile formed on his lips. It was a filthy trick to deny the reader the pleasure of the ending. He had to bite hard on his lip to keep from screaming. He ejaculated a few words indicative of extreme displeasure. He bit his lip a second time to steady himself but it was no use. His hands continued to shake. He let the book drop to the ground. It sprawled there, spine uppermost, the pages spread out face-down like the hands of a yoga practitioner. A spot of blood from his bleeding lip fell and splashed the cover. Tollinger glanced at his wristwatch. The minutes were passing, one by one. If only the

Back indoors, Tollinger unfroze the frame. The actress continued sobbing on the TV screen. "There was no one to tell me right from wrong! No one!"

"Stop crying," the actor said, in a quiet, commanding, but strangely hollow and unfeeling voice. "I love you very much."

18

IT HAPPENED one night that the wild thing fled in secret back to the sea. This poor creature was never seen again, on land or water. It had returned into the ocean's depths, concealed there by wastes of indanthrene blue and shimmering monestial turquoise. Weedy, glistening language trailed out from a colour chart. All that was left afterwards were a few sentences written by a monk, a hooded, tonsured man of whom nothing at all is known except a name. The story, perhaps, no more than utter fiction. Or, if rooted in the real, a distortion. Something exaggerated beyond what's credible. Just as heat on a boiling summer's day can raise up a promontory. Watch it float in the air. Watch as ships can be seen sailing low across the sky, broken loose from gravity, jostling in the restless ether.

If however he existed as a mortal man, presenting himself as some human type of fish, what then? Should we say he was an evil spirit, hiding in the body of a man? A submerged man voicing foreign matter? A demon swimmer? Matter of the sort to be encountered in the life of Saint Audaenus?

It is difficult to say. So many wonders, told by so many speakers, about these rare events. And these rare events are nothing less than the sum of the words in the text.

19

AFTER HIS father's sudden death Tollinger felt joy, guilt, and awe at the efficacy of prayer. This last impression soon wore off. Newly minted prayers for the gift of a model Lancaster bomber, June's return, six packs of ice-cream, a dozen Mars Bars, and impressively good school examination results were repeatedly not answered.

It struck Tollinger finally that his father's death had been a coincidence. No matter. He was cheered by his mother's new warmth. She smiled and laughed a lot.

The End never is. It can bring with it a fresh, bright beginning. Tollinger's mother met Mr Potter. Mr Potter bought Tollinger presents. This back story developed according to the conventions. Mr Potter was a widower. He had money. In time he –

The years passed. Tollinger left home and went to university, after which, like so many graduates, he drifted and zig-zagged like an autumn leaf whirled on a winter wind. And then he joined a band.

"Serious writing takes time," the actor on the screen said. "Time." His face looked enormously thoughtful. Solemnly and calmly, he continued. "Writing a novel takes time. Time."

20

INTERWOVEN FOLIAGE made it dark beneath the tall slender firs. Something pale started out from the shadows before him. It seemed to swim and float down the air. It drifted off through the bars of a gate framed dimly against the sky. He was going downhill, now. There was a gliding motion in the shadows. The text was full of strange rustling sounds. Something sheered in two. The crack echoed.

Tollinger emerged into scenery where the lighting was better. He went past the purple haze of the buddleia, which were the height of his parents. Someone a long way off was playing the Mal Kontents *Greatest Hits* album. Lines from "I'm Not The Same" drifted across the scenery.

I took the blame,
I lost my name,
I left the frame
I'm not the same.

In a spasm of drum beats and squeakily piping organ notes, the music died away. A light föhn wind took up the melody and distributed it among that nearby plantation of tapering firs.

In what had once been the same paragraph Tollinger came across a door in the brick wall. It was freezing cold in the shadow of this wall. He shook all over. It made him regret the lack of a coat.

Tollinger experimentally tried the handle of the door in the wall. He expected it to resist the pressure he'd applied to it but to his surprise the knob turned in his fist. The door creaked open. Its hinges needed oiling.

Tollinger slammed it behind him in the first take, pressing his palms against his ears. In the second take he closed it gently, his hands afterwards remaining at his side. His footsteps fell as gently as snowflakes.

He stepped out into a zone of shining woodland. Here, the trees had slender trunks and luminous silvery bark and were aligned in symmetrical rows. Sunlight on distant water glittered intermittently amid the massed vegetation. A lifelike bird broke noisily from a patch of dark vague undergrowth and fluttered away between the treetops. He had the sudden strange sensation that this was all unreal, something computer-generated. The sensation was one that tingled with the drag of what felt like very tiny fish hooks. It was an odd, wiry feeling. He could hear a distant whirring noise, which ceased.

Cortisone makes one alert and nervous.

He glanced behind him. There was no one around. He touched the nearest tree, which felt solid. So did the red brickwork, which left a smear of pinkish dust on his fingertips. He decided to follow the wall and see where it led.

He went west, with the sun behind him. He felt its warmth on his neck. The shadows cast by the trees were short. It was almost noon. Tollinger followed the wall for two hundred metres or so, until it turned a corner at a right angle and went north. Here, he left the wall and made his way through the silver trees.

Dead vegetation crunched beneath his feet like small bones. He emerged from the woodland and found himself at the edge of a marsh. Reed beds extended to the horizon, dissected by ditches. A swan slowly cruised the nearest ditch, moving steadily away from him. A narrow path snaked between the trees and the marsh. It was brown and well trodden. Tollinger decided to follow it and see where it led. He continued on, northward.

He expected to hear the distant wailing of a siren but the only sound in this quiet place was the *chark! chark!* of a bird. Later, a familiar Red Admiral settled on an unfamiliar blade of grass. Tollinger felt his heart start to thump wildly. He decided to clench his hands. It felt good, the four fingers of his left hand gripped between the thumb and fingers of his right hand. It calmed him a little.

The butterfly soon moved off, zigzagging away. He wondered if orders were being given. Perhaps the orderlies were already on their way. Soon a 4x4 would come smashing through the greenery. A man with a smile and a hypodermic would restore him to obedience. But perhaps it was just a butterfly after all. Like the diagonal reader, security was slow to manifest. No one came. These are trying times yet no one came to seize him. Perhaps he was truly free. Really.

Really!

Tollinger strolled on until he came to hedgerows with cowslips thriving in the verge. A dragonfly with a shining indigo abdomen jerked past. A couple of large fuzzy bees buzzed around his head. He shook them off. The throbbing behind his temple sounded like surf pounding on distant sandbars. How delightful it would be to spend a whole day on the beach, lost in dreams!

The thought made him think of that terrific black and white

movie with Dwight Towers and Moira Davidson. A signal lures you on. The suspense is awesome. A broken message in the night gives you hope.

The thought made Tollinger think of Neil Young's second-best album. "Motion Pictures" had played all through that short hot summer with Vicki Lee Lennox, who preceded skinny Emily, and whom he never talked of to anyone.

The best was *Time Fades Away*.

Meanwhile, behind the privet hedges, there were calendar glimpses of white cottages with red roses curling prettily around small leaded windows. Superfluous primroses added a splash of yellow.

Tollinger mobilised a bundle of aching muscles and achieved a quiet stroll down an English lane. He emerged on to an avenue of villas and mock-Tudor houses. Soon he was in the high street and striding confidently along. Those unmentioned three grams of morphine had put quite a bounce into his step.

He knew where he was going before he went anywhere else. On such a hot dazzling afternoon as this there was a small queue at the quayside. Tollinger went to the office and bought a ticket and joined the day visitors. He'd been nervous that it would be the same ferryman but this one was a much younger man, quite different. He was slim and wearing a check shirt. He whistled cheerily as he took the boat out from the quay, across the estuary.

The other passengers were two elderly couples and a family group with three children. No one took any notice of him. He was the last one into the boat.

It chugged away across the muddy estuary. Tollinger dipped his head, remembering. He felt he'd come a long way to this moment in his life. The past rippled by, in dark waves of remembrance. Old scenery was assembled and dismantled on the great stage of his life.

A hand shook his shoulder

"Wake up, sir! We've reached Bomb Island."

"Eh?"

What had the fellow said?

"We're here, sir. Could you step off the boat please. People are waiting."

Tollinger realised he'd nodded off. The other passengers in the boat were looking at him oddly. The children were grinning. His cheeks reddened. "Sorry."

He was the last one in, the first one off. That was how it worked. He stepped off the gently swaying boat on to the pier. He could hear water slapping below the boards. He stepped on to the island and hurried away, walking fast. He'd soon left the others far behind.

Soon it was as if he had the place to himself. The island stretched away in front of him, devoid of humanity. Gulls passed overhead, screaming. A soft blue mist enveloped the horizon.

He retraced the route he'd taken, passing the museum with the broken sign. He crossed the bridge. The supermarket cart he'd used lay where he'd abandoned it. Tollinger could even see a dark crust of blood coating some of the silver mesh. Further along there were even dark stains on the ground. He must have been leaking badly to have left so much of himself behind. No wonder he'd been light-headed when he'd reached the quayside that night.

He felt good, now. Liberated. In good health. Back in control. He strode briskly on to the bunker. It was there – it existed. The door was half open, inviting him in.

Tollinger wasn't afraid. He couldn't feel the snake. Wherever it was, it wasn't on the island. It wasn't close, he was certain of that. Some strand of snake intelligence still swam in his bloodstream and he sensed it was infinitely remote. Perhaps even now it was wriggling towards Norway. Or wounded and dying in some deep, cold fissure in the ocean bed. Or entombed in an American military research facility, whence it had been transported in a sealed crate, on a huge aircraft. The sealed crate lay in an empty hangar, under armed guard. Upon arrival it was taken in a military convoy deep into the desert. New Mexico, say, or perhaps Nevada. In an air-conditioned basement, deep underground, it was being scrutinised through armoured glass eight inches thick.

Here, in the dark cool empty bunker, all evidence of the elevator which had taken him to the medical unit had gone. It had been done very cleverly. The wall in which it had been set looked old and undisturbed. The ground looked hard and untrodden. It was as if what had happened here had never happened. Clever, that. No doubt if he came back with a shovel and a pick axe he would encounter a slab of unyielding concrete, immensely thick.

He went back to the pier and took the next ferry. This time he had it to himself, apart from the boatman, who was different. This one was thin and old, almost unfit for such employment. He regarded Tollinger morosely and said nothing.

On dry land he did not have to go very far to find a conveyance. There was one parked beside The King's Head. HYPO TAXIS it said across the vehicle's curved rump. A figure sat behind the wheel, head tipped forwards and eyes closed.

Tollinger opened a passenger door and asked the sleeper to take him to Merrivale.

The driver rubbed his eyes and yawned. He looked back at Tollinger, puzzled. "Where?" he said.

"Merrivale. The private hospital."

The driver thought about it for a while, frowning. He had the flushed cheeks of a farmer, and wore a check shirt. At last he said, "Buddy, that place closed years ago."

"It can't have done. I only left it a few hours ago."

The man stared at him. "Buddy, did you say *Merrivale*? D'ya mean the old military hospital? Believe me, buster, it's shut down. It's derelict now." He spoke Manhattan, with a dense Suffolk accent. The vowels dragged, as if the batteries were low.

"Derelict?"

"It's been loik that for a long time. Thoy soy a hotel will be a-built on the site. But they bin a-saying that for years."

The man was mad but that was scarcely Tollinger's concern. "Take me there," he said.

"If you're sure..." the driver replied. He looked doubtful.

"I'm quite sure."

The driver shrugged. "Sure. Okay, pal. Let's hit the highway. Attaboy! Here we go. Up, up, up and away in my beautiful Veyron..."

They soon reached the grounds of the hospital. The driveway had a line of smoky weeds growing down the middle. Knee-high grass lapped at the base of the temporary fencing which barred the old gateway.

The driver braked. "This is the place."

It was, indubitably. Different to how Tollinger remembered it – but nevertheless the place.

He asked the cab driver to wait but the man refused. "You might walk off into that place and never come back," he complained. "Then where would I be?"

Tollinger took out a Franklin. He tore the bill down the middle, retaining the half with the nose for himself and handing the driver an eye, a cheek, a portion of bald head, and some long untidy hair.

"If you wait for me, I'll give you the other half."

"Nuts to you, shamus," the driver said. "This ain't no frigging movie. Gimme the dough, straight."

Tollinger paid him in an acceptable currency. He asked the man for directions back to the town. The driver jerked his thumb over his shoulder, in the direction from which they'd come.

"Just keep walking, mate. Don't take any side roads."

He screeched away, leaving a blue noxious mist drifting across the blacktop. A hedge breathed it in and coughed out three pale moths.

Tollinger walked along the perimeter until he found a hole in the fence. Others had been this way, forcing their way in. The mesh was twisted and flattened down. Feet had crushed the grass and thistles. A blue Cadbury's wrapper had been hooked by thorns. It was trying to wriggle free. Further on Tollinger came across a dead blackbird. Its belly was hollowed out and seethed with white animated maggots. They reminded him of noodle soup.

The narrative sent Tollinger back to the drive and obliged him to crunch along the gravel to the main entrance. The overgrown privet kept reaching out, touching him flirtatiously. The estate's anthropomorphic tendencies were comforting.

Weeds like small wrinkled cabbages sprouted from the pebbles. Each leaf reminded Tollinger of the taut symmetry of an anus.

He found a leather hip flask in his jacket pocket. Emily had given it to him in another age. He took a swig.

Southern Comfort! He hadn't had that in years...

How easy it is, when lacking a photographic record, to forget the naked body of a particular lover. In the absence of spectacular aspects – a missing leg say, or a right buttock bearing a butterfly tattoo, or pubic hair dyed in ginger and scarlet stripes – they blur together, these bodies, do they not? Nipples differ in size and colour but unless you are paying attention and afterwards make notes, they all tend to seem the same.

A jittery butterfly chased the origins of a neurosis on scarlet wings. A silver lager capsule winked. A broken bottle regarded Tollinger wolfishly, with a silent snarl of jagged teeth. The teeth fell apart and an angry mouth shouted, "Twisted fish and a cat's handlebar!" But he had surely misheard.

Misheard? Quite possibly not. Fall made some men tremble and repeat idiotic sentences to themselves. He had never known such men but he had read about them. Besides, was it truly the fall, now? It felt more like being on the cusp of a season, of one sort or another. Or perhaps he'd been tricked in some way, and was actually in Scotland, notorious for its unorthodox precipitation and general anarchy. He'd seen *Valhalla Rising*.

Codeine nagged, fallacies crowded, pathetic. A click in his mind, that's what he sought. Eh?

I cannot cry, I cannot care, no.

So he pressed on, his voice stretched, imitating an old Antony and the Johnsons cover version of a Dylan song.

*

The main building came into view. All its windows were smashed. The place had been blitzed.

Fingers of ivy reached as far as the guttering.

The front door had been removed and lay on the steps, dismembered and charred. An umbrella lay inert there too, its black wings broken. Smashed glass was everywhere. Starfish curled up like poppadoms. Wisps of sea fern bounced by like tumbleweed.

The darkness was waiting for him.

Tollinger made his way into the heart of it.

Once, long ago, Emily had had to spend a weekend at a conference in a Canterbury hotel. He went with her. He remembered that weekend as grey and dispiriting. While she went to lectures and seminars, he went off in search of a grave. He liked tracking down the graves of writers. The ones who lived at the edge. The ones who took a bullet. The ones who drank.

The ones who took hold of language, of form, of expectation, and twisted them into new shapes.

The ones borne down by despair, uncertainty, aesthetic dissatisfaction.

The ones who went to strange places – in their imaginations at least. The ones who were, all along, preparing to leave. Who, in the end, did.

Your heart gives up and gives out.

Others linger on, lusty to the end. And then a cough, a pain in the foot, the back. Concentration fading... Feeling limp. Feeling like a rag. Spirits at about zero. Effort syndrome, of old. Everything behind you, now. The years, heaped up. Your life relived on paper, until you were sick of it. Leaving you, at the end, crying out from a pit deeper than the Hell Gill gorge. Fooling yourself with new beginnings. Making plans to move to a new house, eight miles away, along the Dover Road. Making plans for the next novel. And then that stabbing pain in the chest.

Now your breathing becoming more laboured. The usual

heart flutters, perhaps. Shortness of breath. Chest pains. It's nothing. Take heart!

There's no irregularity in the pulse. And then, an hour or so later, a cry, and you drop to the floor, stone dead.

Tollinger found it in the end, amid all the stone clutter. A big, ugly slab in a nondescript waste of dreary memorials. The writer's name misspelled on the gravestone.

Sleepe after toyle, port after stormie seas... Who could not be pleased by that delicious, drowsy, soporific prospect?

Tollinger went on down the corridor. A floorboard creaked. A voice seemed to cry out from the cellarage. Just a rat, a bat, a bird... When I am old and grey, he thought, I'll watch all those series I haven't yet seen, all the way through from beginnings to middles to ends. *The Sopranos. House of Cards. Game of Thrones.*

Rubbish everywhere. The place had been gutted of its contents, then trashed by intruders. By the look and the smell of the place people came here to piss, shit, booze, take drugs, strip off and fuck.

Something heard his footsteps and fluttered frantically in a far room.

Then silence.

Oddly, he felt no fear. Only a queer tranquillity. There was nothing here that could harm him and he seemed to know it for a certainty. It was written in his blood, in finest copperplate. With lots of stimulants he'd see it all through and enjoy those box sets.

He found his old room. It had been stripped of everything. The place where his bed had been was marked by a shadow outlined on the wall.

He made his way to the control room. Here there was a strange smell of kerosene, dust and mildewed cones.

The screens were gone, everything was gone. The plaster was broken and scarred where the equipment had been ripped out. Lumps of it made the floor uneven. Some of the plaster had melted and fused with the floor. The blobs looked like miniature versions of the stalagmites Tollinger had once seen in a cavern in Sardinia. The memory of that bright distant day was cloudy, though he was certain it involved a boat ride. He had not been with Emily on that day, which spared him a poignant flashback like the ones in *Still Alice*.

Wiring hung loose in clusters, like thin fronds of copper and plastic. A few drops of translucent slime hung from these fronds. The air-con had gone. A dark rectangle enclosing gashes in the wall marked the spot. Beneath the rectangle was an amber puddle.

The scenes he'd been shown in this place still played inside his head. Freckled Shoulder's dialogue was there, too. Tollinger wondered where she was now. In a basement off Whitehall perhaps. He went back up the stairway.

Desolation – you can't beat it, he thought. It's just what happens.

He continued and found the lounge, now just a shell, with every window shattered. The contents were long gone, apart from a monochrome scrap of wrapping from a DVD case. *Haunting, vivid, brilliant, unforgettable* exclaimed dazzled TIME.

Tollinger stepped out into the garden.

The grass and thistles were waist-high and the pathways gone. Or rather those pathways, some of them at any rate, were merely mislaid, for he was able to locate a trickle of bluish gravel which survived under the suffocating press of blades and cramped, jostling stalks.

He waded through the dry green jungle hoping there were no snakes. A mulberry which he did not remember was shedding dark leaves and somehow a crested grebe had jetted in from somewhere. Its presence attracted a robin, which seemed to startle the grebe, which flew off, as did the robin.

He retraced his exit route, with difficulty.

Tollinger went on, into the fast approaching night. It was that time of year, now. Things turned yellow at the edges, then darkened.

Dusk spread its fur over the hedgerows and fields. A strange fluorescent flickering crackled along that distant fuzziness where the land ended and the sky began. He felt a muzziness and smelt a mustiness. He sensed a faint flutter in his stomach, as of something stirring, something awakening from a winter sleep. It must be imagination, he thought. He sweated and shook. It must be – it must be imaginary. He closed it out, that creature uncoiling inside his deepest fear. Don't think of it. Go on, with another story. Something that distracts, something that takes you out of your selves. The consolation of an escape into a different, fantastic world. Hurry into it, and away. Tomorrow! And tomorrow!

He felt his left knee do something as he slipped and almost fell. With a slack, depleted energy he tremblingly recovered his gait. To hell with split infinitives! He went on, into the night. Amphetamines, he decided, would speed matters to a conclusion. He reached for his pills, hoping there would still be some.

And now, out there, the distant island melts in the thickening dark. Somewhere an owl cries out three times, then stops. It's a desolate, cool, melancholy sound, wrenched from the throat of something spectral. As if in response a strange, human wail of pain breaks from the throat of some large animal a short distance away. Tollinger cannot begin to imagine what this random creature might be.

The clear sky is beginning to fill with pricks of light. Tollinger stands there, feeling the chill on his skin. He hears the scratchy whispering of the branches, the hiss of a needle dragging against a vinyl groove. He sees the momentary blur of an expiring meteorite. He's a long way from Hooting Yard, now. Far from so much, so very much.

Night rushes forward and wraps its cool velvet cloak around Tollinger. It's a designer brand, with a famously chic name stamped upon the prose. He nestles snugly amid its comforts.

His lungs inhale a cold frosty sharpness. Up there, across the firmament, a bright company accumulates, like a growing army of dead souls. The Dog Star. The jewels of Orion's Belt, the sparkling outline of the Dragon. The blur of the Pleiades. Arcturus, Altair, Centauri...

But now, out of nowhere, a wind has risen. A rough, coarse, pushing and pulling wind. It drags corrugated sheets of grey across the sky, shuts out the twinkling immensities of space.

Soon grey flakes are settling on Tollinger's scalp and shoulders and breast and on the sleeves of his coat. He stands still, watching his world turn white, unbelievably white. Flake by flake the whiteness spreads out, removing every last prop. One by one the laden trees are airbrushed out. Soon the ground is deep with soft snow.

He's growing thinner and thinner.

Tollinger is just a pair of eyes now, staring out across a featureless waste. Then one eyelid closes, leaving a single staring eye.

It holds a tiny world, with blackness at its centre. The eye jerks shut.

At once it springs open again, as if it's winking.

Part Two

SOMETIMES THE GUIDE urged them on ahead, while he stayed behind to switch off the illumination. And so it was that Tollinger was the first of that small party to cross the narrow bridge over the Mystery River. On the other side they continued, pausing now and again in the immense cavern. The beam of the guide's flashlight rolled across the blackness surrounding them, stopping to pick out a deep crack in a bulge of rock below. It marked where the earthquake had split the foundations of the mountain. They gazed at the fissure, then went on, deeper into the black heart of this place.

The guide stabbed the void with pricks of light. Solemnly this slim serious young man invited them to find meaning amid the billowing misshapen pillars. Abe Lincoln in silhouette! A croc! Silhouettes heightened by hidden lighting and framed by ingenious strokes of shadow. The couple from Nashville chuckled. The couple from Atlanta did not.

Later they paused by a drooping curtain of limestone, beneath which two child actors had once crouched during the filming of a Disney flop.

Tollinger asked the guide if he'd seen *The Descent*, about a bunch of women exploring an unknown cave system and coming up against an underground species of blind, flesh-eating mutant humans.

He said no, sir. He had not.

Very much later in the narrative Tollinger realised he had mispronounced the title. He should have said *The Dee-Scent*, not *The Dissent*.

At THE END of the path, where the cavern expanded and you looked down and across the great basin of glistening, sparkling shapes, the guide, after his spiel, killed all the lights. Now you are in complete darkness and the invitation is: *Listen*. What can you hear? What sound rises to your ears in this cool, calm, immense underground space?

A faint, faint whispering.

A trickle of distant remote laughter.

113

At THE END of the tour the guide unlocked the gate set in the big wall of iron bars. Like prisoners, they were released out into bright daylight.

On and away, down the highway. Tollinger ate pizza at Mellow Mushroom. He felt hollow and hungry. The waitress was as cheery and voluble as a chaffinch. She gave him a tall glass of chilled water, with a long straw, as if he was an infant who had not yet mastered the difficult skill of drinking. The restaurant was space-themed. Connected Rubik cubes were assembled in the shape of a satellite which hung heavily overhead. It unnerved him to be beneath it. He had a hunch he was the only person present who recalled the descent of the chandelier in *Daisies*. And who nowadays remembers that 1938 was the year a chandelier fell on Ernest Hemingway?

Feeling suddenly feverish, Tollinger glanced away. A life-sized helmeted astronaut stood beside the door, flexed to cope with the unfamiliar spring of weightlessness. The pizza was as wide as an auto wheel. The string of cheese topping stretched like an elastic band and wouldn't break. Sweating, scowling, Tollinger raised it higher and higher above his plate. Could this unbreakable cadmium string be a potent clue? Was this the stray, lurid wiring of a synthetic world? Is this just *The Matrix* all over again? Disturbingly, the beer was dark and sweet and nothing at all like Adnams Ghost Ship. Tollinger drained his glass. Still frowning, he noticed there were no dregs. There was nothing there to help him decipher the future.

Next he was inside the CENTER FOR SPACE EXPLOR-ATION. Afterwards Tollinger could not recall how he arrived there. It was not far from Mellow Mushroom, just a few miles away in the adjacent paragraph. Between locations green signs were everywhere, giving directions.

The CENTER FOR SPACE EXPLORATION is marvellous. The very name is like the definition of a novel, Tollinger might have reflected, had he not been distracted by the reflections in the first building's dark sheets of glass. White rockets clustered and shimmered there in fairy wings, like unusual fungi which, if ingested, bring on hallucinations of startling clarity. But that day Tollinger was not in the mood for postmodernist whimsy. He preferred gravely to admire a genuine, original life-size Saturn 5.

You could stand beneath it and hear a recording of the sound of take-off.

You could emulate the first men on the moon by walking along a gantry that led towards the front door of this gigantic tube.

You could admire a robot fish, circling forever its habitat of clear water inside a giant translucent ball.

You could stare through Plexiglas at a Biological Isolation Garment (BIG).

You could try to land on the moon.

You could peer in through transparent panelling at a recreation of Werner von Braun's office and be impressed by the big man's big desk, the white important telephone, the photographs of the great rocket scientist with American presidents.

On modest walnut-veneer furniture were positioned pleasant photographs of von Braun's wife and children, plus a row of model rockets, from Saturn 5 all the way back to the first rocket of the Free World, the V2. The V2's flanks were white and blank, the only missile not to bear the words U.S. ARMY or UNITED STATES.

The military in its contemporary and future incarnations was celebrated at the end. A gleaming Humvee with a small missile launcher atop stood against a theatrical backdrop of bare brown mountains in an arid desert landscape. A drone cut across the sky and robot tanks hurried across the sand. THE FUTURE FORCE... said a sign, exhibiting ellipses, a device Tollinger had always adored. Ellipses indicate all that's unspoken. All that lingers on when speech has died away.

Deployable. Agile. Versatile. Lethal. Survivable. Sustainable.
The glorious thesaurus of future imperial victories.
Exit.
And onward, down Heroes Highway.

Down Ronald Reagan Memorial Road to Slaughter.

Constant incitements to action beside the Interstate. Huge stalks of metal supporting massive screens.

TATTOO REGRET?

WORLD FAMOUS ORANGE ROLLS.

SHRINE OF THE MOST BLESSED SACRAMENT – VISIT OUR GIFT SHOP.

Tollinger refuelled at Good Hope.

Then on, across the massive mud-brown Tennessee, to Carraway Boulevard and all that lies beyond. Munching an Einstein Bagel. Seeing a wild turkey scampering away across the verge, into undergrowth. Taking the A side lane. Taking the 16th Street exit. Seeing flowering dogwood and a mockingbird in Vulcan Park. Observing an American robin, big as a blackbird and just as friendly. Calling by at the café at 1906 1st Avenue North, for steak in gravy and fried green tomatoes. On the menu, oddly: Jew Fish Steak-Potatoes.

The Stars and Stripes fluttered everywhere, as if Americans, roaming the vast expanses of their nation, were fearful of forgetting which country they inhabited. Like early onset dementia patients they benefited from simple reminders and good, honest nudges. The auto number plates brought reassurance. Alabama was sweet and homely. God was quietly commanded to bless these United States, which possessed an equal entitlement to upper-case. A unique selling point is best made snappy.

PATRICIA TODD: FEARLESSLY PROGRESSIVE.

Tollinger tuned into Ninety-Seven Three, The Easy Channel. *The difference is we only play relaxing and refreshing music. None of that annoying hard rock.*

Miranda Lambert sang Greyhound Bound for Nowhere.

Elton John sang Candle in the Wind. The Supremes sang You Keep Me Hanging On. Rod Stewart sang Tonight's the Night. Simon and Garfunkel sang The Sound of Silence. The Beatles sang If I Fell in Love with You. Nilsson sang Without You. Paul Simon sang Slip Sliding Away. Fleetwood Mac sang It Doesn't Matter Any More. The Turtles sang Happy Together. *Songs that bring back great memories from a simpler time.*

Thunder rolled in the green hills all around.

The passage of a recent tornado was marked out by a wide arc of trees flattened with startling symmetry amid a dense, rolling belt of forest.

In a dark room, rain lashing the parking lots, Tollinger watched for the first time *To Kill a Mockingbird*. He felt he knew the actor who played Boo but he couldn't put a name to him.

Hours later, a distant freight train wrenched the night apart with its doleful quartet of stretched-out mournful hoots.

The knob on the cooker offered two choices: HI and LO.

You press wall switches up to turn lights on and down to turn them off. This is England upside down, back to front, in reverse. The steering wheel is on the passenger side. The fast lane is the slowest. A mirror world.

Downtown, few walked. People scampered from asleep cars in parking lots, into offices: and that was it. The streets were as eerily empty as a post-apocalypse disaster epic. Once, by the Alabama Theater, Tollinger encountered a sauntering, sullen individualist with a cigarette dangling from his mouth. The oncoming youth's black T-shirt read NIHILIST. They passed in silence. But out in the hilly tree-lined suburbs there were joggers, mostly tanned, slim young women in shorts, with baseball caps jammed on their scalps and a thin long white wire sprouting from each ear. They ran past him without acknowledgement.

Tollinger, marvelling at everything, went up the elevator beside Vulcan. To the north he could distinctly make out Region Fields. A bright sunlit day, no one else around. It felt like being in a Hitchcock movie. On the high wind-torn platform below the gigantic muscular cast-iron God there would be a struggle. The camera would show the perilous drop. The villain would in due course fall away, getting smaller and smaller. Truth and justice would triumph over deception and un-American values. Tollinger felt fearful and queasy. He had never been good with heights. Plus there was Emily, she was always on his mind, she was always on his mind. He should not have come here. The gusts tugged at his sleeves.

IN A WRECK? NEED A CHECK?

WHEN YOU DIE YOU WILL MEET GOD

UNCONTESTED DIVORCE, $199

At Region Fields Miss Alabama herself appeared, wearing her silver crown. She waved at the crowd, bright with beauty and youth. Tollinger enthusiastically waved back.

Tollinger had more money, now. More than enough for numerous divorces. That forgotten second best Mal Kontents song he'd penned, "Unexpected Surprise", was used as the signature tune for a U.S. cable drama, *Killing Time*. When the series became an unexpected hit the royalties flooded in.

A pretty tale. It balanced that other back story, the dark one, in which Emily aborted Tollinger's child.

Later, the day after she'd seen *Inception*, Emily walked to a footbridge over the roaring, whining North Circular. It was close to the old Crooked Billet site, before that the home of Roger Ascham, tutor to the slippery Queen. In Emily's stained pocket was found an ancient wrinkled non-fiction paperback, *The Sense of an Ending*. "I like *Lost*," her last message to T.

Halfway across she paused, swaying above the fast-flowing machines. Witnesses said Emily appeared intoxicated. Her face shone. She was transfigured by the brilliance of her future. Making a quick calculation, she chose the fast lane and an oncoming heavy goods vehicle. Fury road! A rubbery oblivion.

When he heard, a hole was struck inside Tollinger, enlarging the existing crater. Leftover life to live, now.

"Can't live," the balladeer wailed, "if living is without you." But he could, that was the trouble. The raucous noise of life begins again. Wounded and bruised and aching, he'd endure. Tollinger would go on, as main characters always do. That good-looking savage in *Apocalypto*, for instance. About to be decapitated? An eclipse will intervene. An arrow through the guts? Snap it off! Bashed over the head with a club? Shake that headache away and rise up, sprightly and full of determination. Another arrow penetrating your torso? No matter. Scramble to your feet and stumble onward. Live to kill another day.

PEACE, LOVE & JESUS.

GET FEDERAL PREMIUM AMMUNITION AT LARRY'S PISTOL & PAWN.

Tollinger drove to a shopping mall which rose up out of a glittering ocean of parked cars. For no obvious reason the mall displayed two gigantic wooden horses, each big as a London double decker bus. He went into a large bookstore. To his surprise its enormous multiple shelving units held only one title by Mailer and only two by Updike. But vampires and murder were everywhere. Dust jackets shone with stylish representatives of the undead, who had good bone structure and whose snow-white complexions were nicely suited to swirling purples and buttoned mauve. Crime offered limos in mountain landscapes and long-haired blondes open-mouthed in the presence of giant knuckles clenching stubby hand guns. Snow was prettily sprinkled with scarlet and alleyways held dark shapes.

Behind the check-out, occupying almost the entire wall, loomed a massive reproduction of the lurid cobalt cover of the first edition of *The Great Gatsby*. Tollinger paid for his anthology of F. Scott Fitzgerald stories.

The nurse – her name was Helen Earle – peered about eagerly.

"I don't see anybody," she said. "Except oh, there's Ronald Colman. I didn't know Ronald Colman looked like that."

He read what happened after Scott completed the first chapter of *The Love of the Last Tycoon*. Littauer at *Collier's* was uncertain whether or not he wanted to publish. Littauer asked to see more than the six thousand words he'd read so far. Furious, Scott sent the material to the *Saturday Evening Post*. No go there, either. So he drank, heavily. He denied it, the boozing, to his mistress, Sheilah Graham. But she was suspicious. When he went out for a haircut she went through his bureau drawers and found eleven empty gin bottles. Later she recalled how she said to him: You'll die. You'll drop dead. You'll have a stroke. At least, that's what she claimed she said – long after his death.

Scott told her he considered Dreiser his greatest contemporary.

Sheilah came to Encino one night to find Scott with two bums he'd found on Ventura Boulevard. He'd felt sorry for them, had invited them to dinner, had given them two of his Brooks Brothers suits. Sheilah was angry. She threatened the men with the cops. Scared, the men left. Scott stared blankly. Inside he was angry. Sheilah warmed up some tomato soup and passed it over. Scott picked up his bowl and hurled it against the wall. He slapped Sheilah, hard. He screamed her real name. That was mean.

She wrote that he seemed like a deranged Rumpelstiltskin. She decided to depart. Scott blocked the way. You're not leaving this house, he said.

I hate you! Sheilah shouted. I don't love you any more!

Scott lit a cigarette. You're not going, he said. He added: I'm going to kill you. He opened the table drawer where he kept his gun. It wasn't there. He tore out all the drawers. Where's my gun? he screamed. He phoned his secretary, Frances. Frances, he said. I've been hearing suspicious noises. Have you any idea where my gun is? No, I haven't, Mr Fitzgerald, she replied. Did you see me put it anywhere? Maybe I hid it, he said. No, Mr Fitzgerald. I'm sorry to say I didn't. He hung up. He rummaged among the pots and pans.

I want to go, Scott, Sheilah said.

You're not going, he said. You're not getting out of here alive. The exclamation marks were immense and vivid and deepest black. The mood was ugly. The territory was soap opera.

Scott continued searching.

Where is that goddam gun? he cried.

Sheilah grabbed the phone. She called the cops. The cops said they'd be over. Sheilah walked to the door. She walked out the door. She reached her car. She had trouble starting it. She became hysterical. The car started. Sheilah wept all the way home. As she entered, the phone was ringing in her empty apartment.

In the morning a letter arrived, Special D. Get out of town or you will be dead in 24 hours, it said. She recognised the writing. More letters arrived later that day. Leave town, he threatened, or your body will be found in Coldwater Canyon.

Later Scott apologised. The awful things I said, he wrote. They came from the merest fraction of my mind. I want to die, Sheilah, he wrote. And in my own way. For over two years your image is everywhere.

It's not long now, Scott said.

He never told me that he was writing about me, Sheilah remarked.

Stahr is a lonely man. He is still in love with his dead wife, Minna. Stahr falls in love with an English girl, Kathleen.

Stahr is Scott. Minna is Zelda. Kathleen is Sheilah. Kathleen speaks like me, Sheilah wrote. She uses my phrases. Sheilah was thrilled. He had taken their first meetings and worked magic on them!

I tried to understand the mystery of love, wrote Sheilah.

In Birmingham, in the art gallery down the road from where the bomb went off, Tollinger encountered Georges Merle's startling painting *L'Envoûteuse*. Emily must surely have posed for the artist. The similarity was far starker than anything as flimsy as a resemblance. It made Tollinger tremble. He went out to a bar and drank bourbon. The next day, after a sleepless night, he drove south on Interstate 85, passing en route a gigantic peach and a large Confederate flag flown adjacent to the highway by the Sons of Confederate Veterans. After this there was a sign which showed a scarlet demon flourishing a pitchfork beside the message GO TO CHURCH OR THE DEVIL WILL GET YOU.

Later he found himself going down HANK WILLIAMS MEMORIAL LOST HIGHWAY.

On the Lost Highway he shaped the arid thought that there is one moment in life which is like coming to that page in a book where you reach the final sentence. What's behind it is all there'll ever be and beyond the final speck of punctuation lies only a white emptiness. An emptiness, a void of infinite possibility. An aftermath of time and story in which lies storm or calm, life or death, or something in between, a birth, or even something unimaginable. It's there that the narrative has to run on without you, now.

In Montgomery, Tollinger went via Gatsby Lane to Fitzgerald Road. From there he went via Zelda Road to Zelda Place.

It was a Sunday. He parked by Zelda Cigar and dined at The Egg and I. In the men's room, as he urinated, he was softly serenaded by Simon and Garfunkel.

After brunch and coffee, Tollinger drove on to the Fitzgerald Museum at 919 Felder Ave. *F. Scott Fitzgerald, his wife Zelda and daughter Scottie lived in this house from October 1931 to April 1932. During that period Fitzgerald worked on his novel* **Tender is the Night** *and Zelda began her only novel,* **Save Me the Waltz**, the blue metal plaque informed any passer-by requiring data.

It was a substantial house for three people, located at the corner of two streets, amid open lawn, shrubs and trees, including a large Southern magnolia. Tollinger sat on the third of the five brick steps under the porch, waiting for one o'clock.

He tried to imagine Scott walking up and down these steps, but could not. At five past the curator welcomed him inside.

The curator was in his twenties, slender, bearded. He was an aspiring writer. Impudently, he asked Tollinger how old he was. Startled, Tollinger told him. The curator led him through to a back room and switched on a television. "Watch this," he said.

A documentary rolled. A pleasant, commanding voice ran smoothly through the biography and described the better-known works. Tollinger grew restless, resenting being lectured with dull public facts he already knew. His attention drifted to a side wall and focused on a framed enlargement of an old 23 cent stamp. It bore the head of our rosy-cheeked novelist posed against a distant blob of light reflected in florid water. It was intended, presumably, to evoke the final paragraphs of *The Great Gatsby*. But it seemed to Tollinger to be more redolent of an apocalyptic scene from the brush of John Martin.

Another room displayed paintings by Zelda. Nude, muscular women whose bodies bulged out, giving them a misshapen appearance, cavorted amid anarchic, mysterious settings. They projected a sense of disturbance and wild, dark, erotic energy. She had talent, undeniably, but the exhibition seemed derivative, too full of echoes of Picasso's 1908 nudes and other classic modernist painting. What was revolutionary before the Great War seemed mundane and conservative in its aftermath. It reminded Tollinger of the dull and derivative art he'd seen in the Whitechapel Art Gallery.

The main room of the museum held a variety of memorabilia. Newspaper cuttings testifying to that golden age when an author's wife was newsworthy. A photograph of a short-haired vamp with voluptuous sullen eyes and a ripe sensuous compressed mouth below the headline MRS SCOTT FITZGERALD LEAVES TODAY AFTER VISIT IN MONTGOMERY.

An advertisement in copperplate script: *Three distinguished Judges choose the TWELVE MOST BEAUTIFUL WOMEN using Woodbury's Facial Soup.* One of the distinguished judges was F. Scott Fitzgerald.

Because no other man of his time writes so sympathetically, skilfully, and fascinatingly about women.

A poster for the film *This Thing Called Love*.

A first edition of *Tender is the Night*, which the curator said was a bad piece of writing and which Tollinger hotly asserted was just as good as *Gatsby*.

We had fifty visitors yesterday, the curator said proudly. Seven were from Austria, seven from the Czech republic. Saturday is a good day for visitors. Sunday is not so good. I think we may need to close on Sundays, he said.

The movie *This Thing Called Love* was the last one that Fitzgerald saw. I feel awful, he said as he left the cinema. Outside, he asked Sheilah how he looked. Very pale, she replied.

I did not know that he would die the next day, she wrote.

Tollinger left Montgomery, crossed the Tallapoosa River and came at last to Wetumpka. He had reached the place where he most wanted to go.

Here, to the east of Highway 231, the crust of the republic was disturbed by an ancient turbulence. Tollinger turned off, taking the Harrogate Springs Road across the floor of the gigantic, broken crater. To the north the land was thickly forested, rising steeply up.

After ten minutes or so Tollinger quickly pulled over on to the verge. Here, at last, was a glimpse of the origins of this disfigured place. An arc of rock split the matted vegetation which coated the base of the crater wall. It resembled a scar.

He stepped out of the car and crossed the highway, going a little way up the slope to scrutinise this curve of banded stone more closely. The rock face consisted of a seam of yellow ochre capping a layer of pink streaked with white. It was cracked and fissured by heat and rain, a lingering remnant of the original immense explosive convulsion.

Tollinger stooped to pick up some of the small misshapen pebbles which littered the base of the exposed rock. Each pebble was coated in a pink dust which clung to his skin like talc. One was flesh-red, one grey and the other three were the colour of bone.

He slipped these fragments of the United States into his pocket and went back to the car. He drove on a little way to the Buck Ridge junction. Here Tollinger turned right, braked, reversed, and started the trip back to where he'd come from.

THE END